The Inevitable

Geoffrey John Jacobs

authorHOUSE®

AuthorHouse™ UK Ltd.
500 Avebury Boulevard
Central Milton Keynes, MK9 2BE
www.authorhouse.co.uk
Phone: 08001974150

First published by AuthorHouse   6/16/2011

ISBN: 978-1-4567-7599-5 (sc)

Contents

"And there shall be signs in the sun, and in the moon, and in the stars; and upon the earth distress of nations, with perplexity; the sea and the waves roaring; Men's hearts failing them for fear, and for looking after those things which are coming on the earth: for the powers of heaven shall be shaken."

Luke 21: 25-26   (King James version).

Chapter 1.
Just another day.

Monique Chevalier rose from her slumber, stretched out, fully opened her eyes and muttered to the uninspiring, dispassionate, empty, bedroom..

"Epargnez-moi cette vie que j'ai choisie"

(Spare me this life - I have chosen).

This, despite the Claude Monet prints, outrageous drapes and wallpaper defiantly adorning every wall. A rebellious streak maybe, in one so disciplined.

The hologram still flickered life into the nostalgic images of her late, dancing parents.

Yet again the automatic wake up alarm had failed, and so Monique found herself rushing against time, for she had to make the 10:30am flight to Zone 108 : Cairo.

An intimate relationship, in any guise because of her line of work was totally impractical, for she could never fraternise with anyone, outside the Ministry.

Most of the functions within her apartment were voice controlled, including the shower, music system, life giving coffee machine and 'old faithful', the toaster, with the proviso she had loaded the slices of bread, into the wretched thing.

She marched from room to room barking out instructions, which resulted in a chorus of machines kicking into life, like a good-morning, breakfast symphony.

She had it timed to perfection, had to, for there was never anyone else there to provide support or to whisper, as she left for the day,

"Avoir un bon voyage de retour chérie.

Was there room for romanticism in 2060, or was the world so austere, bleak and dispassionate, that such emotions had become an irrelevant weakness.

She had packed her overnight bag, remembering the temperature extremes in Zone 108 plus, she could always be diverted to another Zone, at very short notice. Often was.

This globe trotting life style has as many disadvantages as it did advantages. Never forgetting the sinister reason behind every journey she and the other Facilitators[1] made, for they had awesome powers and authority.

Often, as she prepared for another escapade, she would reflect on how she became a Facilitator, indeed the very origins of this body of people.

When the Zones were first established there were serious concerns about how law enforcement would be maintained in a situation where every Zone was autonomous. Thus ending mandatory international impositions and codes of conduct.

Because of the civil unrest during the early days of the Zones, there required to be several layers of law enforcement. The simplest form of enforcement was left to traffic management and local community controls, by part-time policeman.

The next level of enforcement was given over to the state police. These are men and women created from many of the servicemen who had been made redundant following the formation of the Zones.

The most militant of the state police were men taken from the SAS, SBS and paratroop regiments. These men would be absolutely ruthless in dealing with any insurrection or civil unrest. Known, as enforcers.

---

1 Facilitator:- Agent of the Zone who investigates potential global threats, at any time, for any reason. They have unlimited power.

The enforcers very soon became feared because they had authority and jurisdiction to impose any level of arrest and incarceration on anyone, they suspected as being a lawbreaker. It was Stop and Search at a very uncompromising order.

Early confrontation came when organised crime in the Zones try to assert their influence previously indulged by corrupt judiciary and government officials.

These nepotistic relationships enabled crime bosses, to avoid punishment, or even arrest.

However, the state police, who were paid amongst the highest wages in law enforcement, had no need to be hesitant with regard to organised crime. They quickly imposed law and order in the criminal fraternity, which inevitably led to many murders during the early years. Enforcement and retaliatory killings on both sides.

The state police initially were required to be accountable to their police masters, for every action they took that resulted in arrest, or where violence was involved. It became apparent that the lawless people in society were using this weakness in the system to exploit opportunities to commit crime.

In Zone 004 (United Kingdom), there was a turning point in the former city of Manchester. When state police were required to investigate a gambling club, where designer drugs were being used. The owner of the club refused to co-operate with the state police and violence ensued.

The violence escalated until weapons appeared. There resulted a fire fight when state police returned fire. This resulted in the final death toll of thirty five including four state police.

The story was hyped up the News press, causing a public outcry. There followed a series of ministerial addresses and discussions in Parliament.

Because of the state of the world, every Zone now had an autonomous parliament but nevertheless still had to take decisions to guarantee the continuing law-abiding requirements of all of its citizens.

In concluding, the Home Secretary of the time, decided that the state police had acted in a defensive manner and that no further action should be taken.

This led to public indignation with social do-gooders insisting the state police were out of control. The response from the government was that the Zone was now operating under a state of zero tolerance.

The idea of non-accountability for extreme police actions horrified many people.

However there soon followed a significant reduction in the number of crimes, from murders, rapes, arson, drug abuses through to petty crimes of shoplifting and street violence.

With these statistics presented back to the public, there were no longer discerning voices claiming loss of state police accountability. For they were being effective.

If the streets are safer, then quite frankly, there is little or no justification in complaining about extreme police brutality. But does that translate into the means always justify the ends. When it comes to a world that has fragmented, requiring every Zone to stand or fall by its own legislation and population control , then yes, of course, it makes absolute sense.

Many Zones had enforced extreme measures when they introduced a new body of men that were classified as State Security. These people were accountable only to the Home Secretary, the Prime Minister, the head of the civil service and certain unidentified cabinet ministers.

This new body would in a previous life have been MI6, in the UK., CIA in USA and FSB in Russia, Mossad in Israel etc. etc They would work in a covert manner and account only to senior people in their native Zone.

This law enforcing model was not adopted globally.

In fact, in Zone 004 the introduction and enforcement of these laws were provocative leading to discontent amongst lawmakers in Parliament. Infringement of civil rights and liberties many would protest.

As before, all protestations were duly ignored.

For a time there existed the three levels of law enforcement, in most Zones. What was now needed would be a body of people who transcended even this structure. Their purpose would be to operate internationally. As 195 countries had become 147 Zones, there required to be an international police force.

To bring this into existence, there were many meetings with senior government officials from most of the 147 Zones. The remit for the Facilitators, as they would be called, would be to scour the world going to any Zone to check for illegal or potentially hazardous activities.

It was not that the Zones were seeking an utopian global culture. They just needed to as certain as they could, that if mankind cannot live in harmony, then at least totally irresponsible actions would be identified, ended and the perpetrators severely punished.

This was the only way the Zones could co-exist whilst in isolation. An oxymoron if ever there was one.

This new and powerful group of people trained and funded by all Zones became known as the Facilitators.

Their selection and training proved as colourful and challenging as the forming of the group itself.

Some argued men only. Other's that only having macho, bullshit, testosterone, Neanderthals, would start problems, not fix them.

So what skills and capabilities would the Facilitators require. Multi lingual, high I.Q., excellent health in mind and body, adaptability and flexibility, strength of character and the ability to be absolutely ruthless.

Candidates would be taken from both sexes within an age band of 25 to 40 years. Initially the selection was made from known members of organised bodies from the military, state police and retired security operatives.

Next to the universities and students on post graduate PhD's. Government scientists, mathematicians, physicists, doctors, psychologists and lecturers.

The selection process took a disproportionally long time and after a year most Zones had less than fifty potential Facilitators. Things moved on from there, thankfully.

To be a Facilitator, no easy matter Monique reflected.

As the basic entry level of education for all Facilitators was a traditional University degree, even though global higher education standards were thought by many to have been one of the major casualties, following the formation of the Zones.

However the disparities across the world became very evident when a degree obtained in one Zone was challenged in other Zones.

Facilitators in the early days found the intellectual capabilities of certain Facilitators far exceeded that of others. That situation was untenable.

Minimum Educational Standards (MES) were introduced globally for Facilitator selection in the form of very demanding entrance examinations.

The selection tests covered languages, mathematics, visual response, problem solving, memory retention capability, lateral thinking, inter personal skills in particular communication, body language, attitude and responsiveness during extremely stressful interviews.

Physiological and psychological profiling. Behavioral abnormalities. Family history. Full DNA and health profiling. Physical fitness testing including the ability to cope with extremes of temperature, height, depth, and physical disorientation.

They had to be able to swim two kilometres, climb, abseil and complete three solo parachute jumps. All tests considered essential, for character assessment.

The MES programme was introduced retrospectively in 2022 resulting in many previously accepted and trained Facilitators being re-evaluated; with some being dismissed from the service.

The MES was soon adopted globally, as the 'Standard'. This brought a sense of equality to all Facilitators underpinning their working relationships. Mutual respect at last prevailed.

The embarrassment of occasionally having inferior Facilitators had been addressed and their status and reputations benefited accordingly.

For international learning opportunities the position for centres of learning excellence became untenable with many of the most prestigious universities now only providing learning to their indigenous population. Cultural integration could only be found from students who became residents, before the Zones were formed.

Many lamented this as the world became more isolated, as Zones. It seemed also unfair that the majority of prestigious universities were to be found in the USA.

University & Location	Founded
Massachusetts Institute of Technology - Cambridge, MA	1861
Stanford - Stanford, CA 94305	1891
Harvard - Cambridge, MA 02138	1636
Universidad Nacional Autonoma de Moxico - Mexico City	1910.
Berkeley - University of California	1897
Peking - located in Beijing	1898
Pennsylvania - Philadelphia, PA 19104	1740
Cornell University - Ithaca, New York	1865
Shanghai Jiao Tong University - Shanghai China	1896
Yale University - New Haven, Connecticut	1701

These same universities appear time and again for medicine, engineering and business and along with the main banks and finance institutions, have been the real power base throughout the USA and the world.

For many years conspiracy theorists believed these academies have had considerable influence around the world, in politics, the military, financial and commerce.

Reminiscing over, packed and refreshed, Monique left the apartment, setting the alarm system to maximum surveillance, both by voice command and remotely as the apartment integral sensors constantly monitored her every movement, including ingress and egress.

The apartments occupied by all Facilitators had unparalleled levels of security which had never been compromised. Not that any Ministry of Security would report any such event.

In this bleak Zone, like so many others, intolerance of failure would result in punitive punishments, from indeterminate prison sentences to death. The reasons and justification for this draconian uncompromising law enforcement, were no longer questioned.

No one dared.

The silent ride to the airport in the hydrogen powered Ministry car, gave time for reflection, as she gazed through the one way windows, into the near deserted streets. The pictures and stories she had read, captured by period photographers, authors and artists, long past, still fuelled her imagination.

She had also been recently reminiscing about her parents and her upbringing. A chemist for a Father and a psychology lecturer for a Mother. Having no siblings, she had been part raised by relatives in her birth town of Mantes-La Jolie, sixty kilometres North West of Paris.

Photographs, holograms, videos, taped telephone messages and digitised audio-visual recordings, served as the only continuing memory of relatives, long since seen, or even contacted.

As a Facilitator she had authority to travel the world, but each trip had to be sanctioned at the highest level, also during each trip her movements were monitored literally for every minute.

Slipping away from a project to visit an aging aunt, would result in a major security alert with repercussions. Also all Facilitators had two personal bodyguards, who travelled with them to Zones when on assignment.

Monique had been brought to the UK in 2025, aged six, at the start of the world reorganisation from countries to Zones. The disintegration of the world had been progressing since 2015 after the foiled attempt by terrorists to contaminate the water supplies at:-

Damn name	Location.
Syncrude Tailings Dam	Canada
Chapetón dam	Argentina
Pati dam	Argentina
New Cornelia Tailings	United States
Kambaratinsk Dam	Kyrgyzstan
Bakun Dam	Malaysia

by using a mixture of Sodium Fluoroacetate (Compound 1080), Dioxin, Anthrax and Botulinum. This lethal concoction was to be introduced into the dams using remotely controlled miniature aircraft. The aircraft skin would dissolve on impact in the reservoirs, releasing the lethal cargo.

Their reason. Specifically to promote international terrorism. Such was the shock to the world that this outrage had been planned, that repulsive disgust permeated through every country, showing terrorism would destroy the human race, for it's own ideology. The result, most terrorist groups were hunted down to extinction, even by their own families. An irony so profound and with a devastating long term impact.

Global warming and weather extremes, only added to the unsettled state of the world. With each country providing help only to its indigenous people, whether suffering devastation from tsunamis, earthquakes, hurricanes, floods, droughts, famines and disease.

They all stood alone as Zones. No more global support.

This self protectionism really grew after the Haiti disaster in 2009 when billions of dollars were given from around the world and still the population continued suffering for years from corruption and greed. This had happened so many times before and since, with international aid being diverted by corrupt politicians.

Nation after nation bore testament to the vile selfishness in mankind. The churches throughout the world were just a culpable and charitable organisations ended.

Corrupt politicians and escalating organised crime only fuelled the fear and distrust, and government agencies from the national police to special departments became powerless. This became particularly evident in 2054 when banned drugs reached epic proportions and crime rocketed out of control in nearly every Zone.

Absolute anarchy ensued, with religion losing any credibility on the discovery that the Vatican had amassed billions of dollars worth of diamonds, pure gold, enriched uranium and cocaine.

Belief in any deity became irrelevant and pointless.

There followed many desperate attempts at regaining control, as the horrors of the 1917 Russian revolution and the 1478 Spanish Inquisition became a reality. Governments faced melt down and anarchy.

Human Rights had been abandoned along with religion and international courts. The history books tell us that from the late 1990's to 2040, individuals could take their concerns to The International Court of Justice, the primary judicial organ of the United Nations.

Based in the Peace Palace in The Hague, Netherlands, its main functions were to settle legal disputes submitted to it by states and to give advisory opinions on legal questions submitted to it by duly authorized international agencies, and the UN General Assembly.

The U.K. Human Rights Act 1998 aim was to make available in UK courts a remedy for breach of a Convention right, without the need to go to the European Court of Human Rights in Strasbourg.

It also abolished the death penalty. However, this was reintroduced in 2035 as a drastic measure to re-establish crumbling authority. By 2045 every Zone had a capital punishment programme re-established.

Those executed were never identified and the judicial processes, never reported. Philistine, uncompromising and relentless law enforcement. Without human rights.

As unbelievable as it may seem, reflected Monique, well into the 21st century, an individual could take their grievance to the Strasbourg court.

How things have changed to this realisation of the terrifying predictions given in the Nineteen Eighty-Four dystopian novel by George Orwell, about the totalitarian regime of the Party.

The story depicts an oligarchical collectivist society where life in the Oceanian province of Airstrip One, is a world of perpetual war, pervasive government surveillance, and incessant public mind control. The individual is always subordinated to the masses, and it is in part this philosophy, which allows the Party to totally manipulate and control humanity.

So from fiction to horrifying fact, as, in the ensuing years, the world managed to disintegrate into the soul less collection of totally autonomous Zones, ensnared by such paranoia. Academics and intellectuals in every Zone who deliberated and pondered their consciences, were always left, literally helpless and unheeded.

With this New World Zonal Order it became imperative that Governments could control the masses. One such control was Electronic Mind Control via 'Cell Phone' Towers

This equipment had been erected and installed with the hidden purpose of exerting mind control over the entire population. Everywhere ELF/ microwave transmission towers and antennas were erected.

The frequency band chosen for cell phones, use second order waves, that Wilhelm Reich discovered in 1948 would effect thought transmission and allow the mind to be manipulated without the victim realizing it.

Reich worked on this project secretly for the CIA from 1947-1952, until he realized who the CIA was planning to use the mind control on, the American people. That realisation cost him his life. But the systems remained.

As soon as people started to understand what was happening, they found a way of disabling the ELF towers from exerting their mind control functions by placing a simple device known as an orgone generator near these towers.

The microwave towers were used in conjunction with HAARP based technology to not only affect subliminal mind control influences, but also to control the weather.

In Zone 001 (USA) the technology had been perfected under the High-frequency Active Aural Research Program (HAARP) as part of the ("Star Wars") Strategic Defence Initiative (SDI). HAARP has been fully operational since 2024 with the ability of potentially triggering floods, droughts, hurricanes and earthquakes.

From a military standpoint, HAARP was a weapon of mass destruction. Potentially, it constitutes an instrument of conquest capable of selectively destabilising agricultural and ecological systems of entire regions.

Other manipulation controls include population reduction by chem-trail spraying operations which take place daily over the skies in many Zones.

Mass surveillance is the pervasive surveillance of a Zone's citizens, to purportedly protect them from terrorists, criminals, or political subversives but realistically mainly to maintain social control.

That led to a totalitarian state where political dissent was crushed by COINTELPRO (counter intelligence programmes). Also known as an Electronic Police State.

In Zone 004 the government and BAE Systems used drones for surveillance including an array of unmanned aerial vehicles, with monitoring equipment such as high-definition cameras, radar devices and infrared sensors cruising at 20,000 feet. They were mainly intended for event security but increasingly, for covert urban surveillance.

All Zones held hundreds of millions of fingerprint and DNA samples on the National DNA Databases.

This level of control and population monitoring has biometrics in schools, even affecting young children.

Other monitoring and control systems include advanced speech-to-text programs (so that phone conversations can be monitored en-masse by a computer, instead of requiring human operators to listen to them. Also social network analysis software to monitor groups of people and their interactions with each other, and "Human identification at a distance" software which allows computers to identify people on surveillance cameras by their facial features and gait. This was named "Terrorism Information Awareness".

Traffic cameras, which were meant to help enforce traffic laws at intersections, also sparked controversy, due to their use by law enforcement agencies for purposes unrelated to traffic violations.

The Indect Project ("Intelligent information system supporting observation, searching and detection for security of citizens in urban environment") develops a intelligent urban environment observation system to register and exchange operational data for the automatic detection, recognition and intelligent processing of all information of abnormal behaviour or violence.

Indect project is for the implementation of a distributed computer system that is capable of acquisition, storage and effective sharing on demand of the data devices used for mobile object tracking, a search engine for fast detection of persons and documents based on watermarking technology used for semantic search.

Continuous and automatic monitoring of public resources such as CCTV, websites, internet forums, usenet newsgroups, file servers, P2P networks and individual computer systems

Global Position Satellite (GPS) technology (progressive satellite launches 1989 - 1991) enabled a system of navigation, accessible by the whole world using a constellation of thirty two near space satellites, orbiting the earth. This system had been hijacked by numerous governments for surveillance and population monitoring. Though globally decommissioned the Zones still had selected services, available to a few.

The command centre for the GPS system is located at US Air Force Base Schriever, 2nd Operations Squadron, of the 50th Space Wing, of Air Force Space Command.

located in Colorado. USA. It is permanently manned using sophisticated technology, to fully maintain and update the GPS system.

The technology, which uses tri-angulation, relies on micro second precision for time and positional accuracy within a few centimetres, for each satellite.

Each satellite has three on-board atomic clocks which are frequently updated from the Master Atomic Clock, located at Schriever.

Orbital decay and positional shift due to gravitational forces from the sun, moon and earth, means every satellite has to be regularly synchronised and re-positioned, to maintain system accuracy. Critical for the end user. Originally it was used not only for domestic locational needs but by the military, agriculture, fishing, rescue services, aviation, traffic management, rail networks, sea navigation.

Considering the extent to which Governments in every Zone had gone to monitor and control their populations still seems incredulous. The cost, complexity and practical benefits, seemingly unjustifiable.

The collective reasoning that survival required total compliance to the dictates of the Zone, meant reason and compromise were always seen as capitulation and weakness. Compliance without protest. Conform or else.

As countries became Zones the strategic defence alliances became irrelevant and government after government pursued the Deterrence Theory, developed during the late 1990's. A bizarre strategy by which governments threaten an immense retaliation if attacked, such that aggressors are deterred if they do not wish to suffer great damage as a result of an aggressive action.

Weapons of mass destruction, conventional weapons, economic sanctions, or any combination of these, can be used as deterrents.

Mutually Assured Destruction (MAD) is a form of this strategy, which came to prominence during the Cold War, (1950 to 1990), when it was used by the US to characterize relations between the United States and Soviet Union. Both nations were prepared to fight a full scale conventional war, but were not willing to risk the carnage of a nuclear war.

This mentality pervaded through the 2040's, creating unparalleled tensions causing the collapse of international harmony and co-operation.

Russia had been uncharacteristically silent and continued with commercial growth from gas and oil supplies across Europe. Very lucrative and threat free.

It had become so engulfed in gain that the armed forces became seriously depleted.

The creation of Zones however crippled Russia economically overnight. So they returned to Stalinism.

The unsettled Iranian threat became a reality when it released a small nuclear device near the Chinese border. That brought such a devastating reaction that Iran immediately ceased all nuclear development, testing and production, even for energy generation.

It became a nuclear impotent country overnight, after China amassed an army on their shared border, threatening a full invasion.

Totally illogical xenophobia permeated across the planet

All this led to the Facilitators and the D.D.1. world-wide indoctrination for survival.

With the airport only minutes away, Monique mused, could it be possible that men, women and children roamed freely, oft times accompanied by leashed dogs, with an variety of birds on the wing.

This situation apparently occurred across the world and yet these many historical references talk of a world where the endless variety of life forms and living styles, challenged the contemporary imagination and exercised the imprisoned memory.

And now, in this monochrome 2060 world, a lifeless existence of control and order percolates through the peoples in every Zone.

This awful transition really started in 2025 following the Iraqi war of 2003 and the Afghanistan deadlock in 2010 with a futile attempt by the UN to destroy terrorist training camps and insurgency. That campaign cost countless lives and lasted until 2018.

The UN capitulated after the foreign military policy of the USA became ridiculed.

The outcry of another Vietnam War, (1955, - 1975) caused the first black President of the USA., to resign leading to a coalition of Republicans and Democrats.

The spectre of 9-11, (11th of September 2001), when Al-Qa'ida, Islamist militants, forced two aircraft to fly into the World Trade Centre, in New York, ceased to inhibit the American people, as they counted their dead and could see no cessation of war.

What followed was an unprecedented period of brinkmanship, sanctions, financial starvation of third world countries and mindless threats of nuclear exchanges. The world became paralyzed regarding trade, commerce, politics and even unrestricted movement of people.

The world effectively metamorphosised from 195 countries into 147 totally autonomous Militarised Zones. Most difficulties were seen in those countries with shared borders and nomadic populations.

It is probably true to say there are no pragmatic solutions only a mute acceptance within each Zone, of the pretence of control.

As the world is in a paranoid state, countries become Zones that are totally preoccupied with protection from each other. Each country is now a designated Zone, numbered 1 – 147.

All the major powers have identified Facilitators, a group of people who, by globally mutual consent, can travel to any Zone, unannounced, to identify the latest threat of hostilities. This includes weaponry, germ and chemical warfare, psychological manipulation, ethnic cleansing, physical disease proliferation and food and water contamination.

Inevitably, even within the Facilitators, there is the emergence of corruption fuelled by power, wealth, religion, territorial gain and politics. So each Facilitator has a unique identification scanning system implant.

Their biometric readings, coupled with DNA identification and a frequently changing electronic code, combine to make each Facilitator absolutely unique and unable to be copied, replicated or cloned.

This extreme security is essential for they have unrestricted access to any Zones inner most secrets. As a Facilitator enters a country, they are physically scanned. Each Facilitator is then monitored by satellites giving a double tri-angulation pin point location trace, accurate to within one metre.

Facilitators have sophisticated communicator devices that continuously monitors their biometric reading. It is also a panic/attack defence alarm. This action not only sends out an SOS via satellite (Globe-Net) but will also cause the Facilitator to pass into a deep near coma sleep, of indeterminate duration.

Their only recovery has to be by a Ministry scientist.

The acceptable code sequences for each Facilitator are housed in Zone computers which are linked through the world wide web with an encryption system devised by a team of top experts in 2125 based on Asymmetric key cryptography, AES and the higher quality asymmetric ciphers. The team was codenamed "D.D.1. 2125".

The team members of D.D.1. 2125 were never introduced but each was given a requirement specification which they developed and downloaded into the Super Computer mainframe. Incredibly sophisticated algorithms resulted and the code generators produced the code sequencers, installed in each Facilitator and into the security assessment computer of each country.

This security system is known simply as D.D.1. (Doomsday Defence. 1.).

Hacking and system compromise is impossible, for every country in the world has micro-second monitoring of D.D.1 for any unscheduled activity.

It is rumoured that the security system experts in 2125 were progressively eliminated, though this was never substantiated, though highly likely.

D.D.1. maintenance, fault fixing, modification and updates are never required with many built in layers of fail-safe and anti corruption and a four level power input standby system, from dedicated nuclear generators.

The D.D.1. system works so effectively because every country wants it to work for their own protection and ultimate survival.

The fifty minute drive to the airport passed quickly, as Monique considered the latest intelligence she had about the four nuclear power stations and the infrastructure supporting these, that she was to visit in Zone 108.

With just four flights a day, airport formalities were minimal plus with her very high level of security clearance, meant she was soon in the departure lounge.

Airport manual security had long since been discontinued as high powered scanning systems using dated but still effective MRI technology, checked passengers, as they travel through the airport.

Remember, that only a few selected people could travel outside of their own Zone and accordingly all those authorised to travel, had a unique identification implant.

This gave a very detailed readout of essential individual data and meant passports, were now obsolete.

Gone were retina and body skeletal scanners, finger prints, DNA random testing. All now defunct.

The idea of extremists trying to sabotage any aircraft had long since ended.

For if such an event was discovered the retribution on the individual, their families and members of any sponsoring organisation, would be extreme.

Every Zone had their own security forces who mercilessly imposed law and order, at their own discretion, that was applied without external comment or judgement. The entire world was in a state of Cold War and self determination.

The growth of secularism in the face of this stark, bleak world cut deep into fundamental beliefs and ideologies.

The work of the Facilitators always has to be mindful of a Zone's remaining religious and political convictions.

Zone 108, is predominantly Islamic, with Muslims following Sunni Islam and Sufi orders and with a minority of Shia. There are also Egyptian Christians.

Monique had given little thought to the disingenuous religions of the world. She hadn't realised how diverse religion was and for her, or any Facilitator to be knowledgeable of these religions, would be absurd.

Christianity : Islam : Hinduism : Buddhism : Chinese folk religion : Shamanism : Animism : Baha'i Faith : Judaism : Sikhism : Shinto : Spiritism : Taoism

With so many conflicting religions permeating across the world, the concept of any religion continuing to be relevant to the survival of mankind became discredited.

A total refusal to compromise on ideology and doctrine led more and more religious groups to revert to fundamentalism and extreme behaviour. They hoped this would give more credence to their particular religious fervour. It very evidently, did not.

The sickening concepts of ethnic cleansing and suicide bombers made even the lightest levels of constructive dialogue impossible. The political and religious leaders pursued such extreme dogmatism and brinkmanship that anger and disbelief preceded meeting after meeting of those seeking world peace, through compromise.

Yet Monique must be sensitive to those choosing to retain faith, for as brutal as the world had become, there will always be passions and convictions denying logic.

If anything, she found herself caught in a triangle of beliefs: Atheism, The Ethic of Reciprocity and Secularism, with the latter most compelling.

A cocktail of beliefs could easily lead to a mind set of irreligion, as abstract and non committal as that was.

Still she remembered a quotation from The Dalai Lama: *"Every religion emphasizes human improvement, love, respect for others, sharing other people's suffering. On these lines, every religion had more or less the same viewpoint and the same goal."*

However her job, as with all Facilitators, frequently requires a dispassionate, pragmatic approach that could have a devastating impact on those deemed to have violated global dictates. Explanations and excuses from those found guilty would not be tolerated and extreme retribution, would quickly follow.

This was the dichotomous creature Monique has chosen to become and yet all of her experiences to date could not possibly have prepared for what would happen soon.

Chapter 2.
Cairo.   Zone 108, Egypt. .

Flight time just three hours, in these high performance jets with hydrogen boosters, designed to shorten journey time and save fossil based fuel.

The Arrivals Suite is a small fortress manned by heavily armed guards, scanners, one way mirrors and impenetrable barriers, leading to the identification and if required, interrogation chambers.

Monique had passed through this security screening ritual so many times, it had become routine, as the dispassionate guards viewed her with sharks eyes.

No words of welcome, just a lifeless gesture to advance to the disembark-ation exit.

The doors opened and the blinding Cairo daylight stabbed into her eyes. Fuck ! cursed Monique and quickly rummaged through her shoulder bag for the essential eye protectors.

"Monique" called Aaheru, though hardly the Chief of Terrors, but one of the nicest guys you could meet and yes, another Facilitator. A warm handshake and embrace followed by a short walk into the waiting, air conditioned car.

Keen to discuss the assignment, Aaheru started to outline the visit programme but was stopped with a gesture of a finger to her lips, indi-cating, silence preferred.

"Later", whispered Monique, "and particularly when we can be certain of complete secrecy".

Her caution was renown throughout the world of Facilitators, which somehow seemed in conflict with her beauty, and gentle manner.

Monique had been chosen for this particular assignment precisely because of her tenacity and resilience.

Her utter refusal to be compromised or deflected and yet, she could charm the humps off a camel. She was loved and feared, but always respected.

So many Middle Eastern countries thrived on their mischievous characteristics, on their ability to beguile, lie, cheat and contradict. Zone 108 excelled in these respects and took pride in doing so.

Her selection therefore made eminent sense, and the Zone 108 authorities knew that.

So, an agreed period of silence and site seeing, as the Ministry car sped silently to their hotel. The World may have torn itself apart but affluence and decadence still pervaded in every Zone.

History is never changing. Forever it is those who have, and those who have not and for Zone 108, no exception for the desperately poor population majority.

Their hotel would have boasted a six star rating in previous years, and though guests were scarce, the quality throughout was of the highest standard.

However, this is not a holiday, Monique quickly reminded herself. The assignment security brief carried sinister undertones, that she and Aaheru were required to thoroughly investigate.

The focus of their investigations were four Generation 7, nuclear power stations across Zone 108 with the first one having been completed in 2025. The technologies employed are Boiling Water Reactors and Pressurized Water Reactors.

The urgency of the security concerns required the two Facilitators to report to their respective Ministries their initial findings within days, not weeks.

Their opening visit was to the original power station, located at the Mediterranean coastal area of al-Dabaa, for it is here that most concerns have been expressed by Zone Security Ministries, in particular Zone 004 (GB) and Zone 001 (USA).

Intelligence reports of misappropriated enriched weapons-grade uranium, had been received by several Zones and though challenged, no conclusive evidence for or against, was not forthcoming. Thus the visit by Monique and Aaheru, to investigate these allegations.

Monique unashamedly admitted her knowledge of the technical aspects of this investigation was limited.

Aaheru explained that enriched uranium is where the percent composition of ^{235}U has been increased through the process of isotope separation. Natural uranium is 99% ^{238}U isotope, with ^{235}U only constituting about 0.711% of its weight. ^{235}U is the only isotope existing in nature that is fissile with thermal neutrons.

Enriched uranium is a critical component for both civil nuclear power generation and military nuclear weapons. International Atomic Energy Agencies monitor and control enriched uranium supplies and processes to ensure nuclear power generation safety and curb nuclear weapons proliferation.

The ^{238}U remaining after enrichment is known as depleted uranium (DU), and is considerably less radioactive than even natural uranium, though still very dense and extremely hazardous in granulated form useful for armour-penetrating weapons and radiation shielding. There was a time when 95% of the world's stocks of depleted uranium remained in secure storage.

Basic technical lecture over, Monique and Aaheru spent two days in secrecy, reviewing the information each had been given. This listed all personnel in the power station including ex employees. Next came contractors and suppliers, from engineers, administrators, to caterers.

Aaheru, an engineer and scientist, then concentrated on the operating control policies and procedures.

Though well documented, the work procedures were never referenced by any one, particularly the plant security department. His enquiries took him over the entire, vast and complex plant.

Monique went straight for the senior management team, demanding proof that every gram of uranium, enriched or otherwise, could be accounted for, with regard to production, storage, usage and disposition.

Came the first casualty of this investigation, when the Operations Director resisted Monique's enquiries, rebuffing the insinuation of lost control and failing accountability.

Twice Monique asked him to demonstrate the operating systems and to provide evidence of material control.

On the third attempt Monique turned to the CEO of the plant to order Zone 108 Ministry Security take the Operations Director into custody. Within one hour, he was gone. This left the Directors in no doubt of the absolute authority of the Facilitators. If proof were ever needed, mused Aaheru.

Resistance or prevarication was no longer seen or heard, at any level, at the plant.

Now the meaningful investigations began with reports flowing back to Zone 004 and Zone 108 Ministries.

After a week of questioning, interrogation, objective evidence gathering, physical examination of equipment, and endless scrolls of documented and electronic records, little progress had been made as to whether any enriched uranium was in fact missing.

Contact with their Ministries through heavily encrypted dedicated computer lines produced no further input or ideas. So why do their masters think uranium, enriched or otherwise has been taken from these power plants, when, by whom, for what purpose, how transported. So many questions.

Aaheru concentrated on how any misappropriated enriched uranium would have been moved, as transportation has to be an integral part of the nuclear fuel cycle.

There are well established, totally secure specialised facilities developed in various locations around the world to provide fuel cycle services along with the transport infrastructure, for nuclear materials.

Most transports of nuclear fuel material occur between different stages of the cycle, but occasionally a material may be transported between similar facilities. With some exceptions, nuclear fuel cycle materials are transported in solid form, the exception being uranium hexafluoride (UF6) which is considered a gas. Most of the material used in nuclear fuel is transported several times during the cycle. Transports, often international, are often over large distances. Nuclear materials are always transported by specialised, secure companies.

Nuclear materials are radioactive. Therefore packaging for spent fuel and high-level waste nuclear materials includes shielding to reduce potential radiation exposures. To limit the risk, containers known as 'spent nuclear fuel shipping casks', are used which are designed to maintain integrity under any condition.

Further complications arose when Aaheru wanted to have a direct sighting of the enriched uranium without having risk to himself and others. Even the wearing of a heavy duty radioactive proof suit was initially unacceptable to the plant management. Their minds were quickly changed.

It was understood that to establish quantities, certain considerations were necessary.

The irradiation of highly enriched uranium in a reactor is reflected in changes of the weight fractions of the uranium isotopes and in the ratios of the initial and post-irradiation amounts of uranium and its isotopes.

The weight fraction of ^{235}U in uranium (w5), the ^{228}U weight fraction (w6), the ratio w6/w5, the 235U weight ratio (U50/U5) and the ^{236}U weight fraction at (w50/w5) may be considered as irradiation parameters.

The irradiation of fuel batches in one reactor core will vary over a limited range and within this range, sets of values of two irradiation parameters, measured after dissolution may be related by simple linear expressions.

This was getting too complicated and involved for Aaheru to comprehend and then comment upon. Yet the exact science needed to establish available quantities of uranium, was central to their investigation.

Detailed data was reviewed for every batch produced since the plant opened in 2025. The amount of power produced exactly corresponded to the enriched uranium depletion to D.U. status. Another approach was to examine the records for every time the nuclear reactor was shut down for maintenance. Some reactor fuel rods would also be changed and engineers would service the water transfer systems, safety detection and insulation equipment.

To shut down the reactor was a very time consuming process, closely monitored for every second. It was just not possible for anyone to take any amount of uranium.

Then news, that shattered every conclusion thus drawn. Security police in Zones

093 India

076 Bangladesh

059 Philippines

128 Vietnam

111 Sri Lanka

067 Nigeria

132 Pakistan

099 Indonesia

reported intercepting significance quantities of enriched uranium all with the same signature and batch traceability code. All had come from this plant, over a period of six months, since January 2059. This enriched uranium was weapons grade, to a standard requiring little engineering to produce nuclear explosive devices.

This revelation put all Zones, on Priority 1 alert. So what the hell was going on.

To many questions, no clues, no reasons, or suspects, absolutely no answers and how much more ^{235}U was to be found in other Zones.

Speculation included it was not a global exchange of nuclear devices but possibly a series of Zonal suicides with indigenous groups producing devastating weapons for self destruction.

Remember no free passage or open borders existed. Only Facilitators and very senior Zone politicians could occasionally travel. But the thought of them transporting enriched uranium in the attaché cases was total absurdity. Even for limited Dirty Bomb production.

If this E.U. were to be made into nuclear bombs then in the present locations, forgetting the physical impact, the combining radioactive fallouts would blanket the world through the winds and weather patterns ensuring no one survived. With no chance of subterranean survival, the world would be contaminated for centuries.

Monique and Aaheru visited the other three power plants in Zone 108 and once again they were unable to substantiate if any uranium was unaccounted for, as they encountered the same very stringent control and accountability systems in place. So how confident were they that all uranium could be accurately accounted for.

Nuclear forensics and attribution had long since been established in the fight against illegal smuggling and the trafficking of radiological and nuclear materials.

These include materials intended for industrial and medical use (radiological), nuclear materials such as those produced in the nuclear fuel cycle, and much more dangerous weapons-usable nuclear materials, plutonium and highly enriched uranium.

Livermore [2] scientists are among the leaders in nuclear forensics, the chemical, isotopic, and morphological analysis of interdicted illicit nuclear or radioactive materials and any associated materials.

---

2 The Lawrence Livermore National Laboratory. California. USA.

They support the national effort in nuclear attribution, which is the challenging discipline of combining input from nuclear and conventional forensics to identify the source of nuclear and radiological materials and determine their points of origin and routes of transit.

Nuclear forensics and attribution go beyond determining the physical, chemical, and isotopic characteristics of intercepted nuclear or radiological materials. Knowledge of the pathways involved in transporting the material is vital to non-proliferation and counterterrorism.

However, strict accountability had been lost soon after the Zones had been established, for power generation required only low grade uranium and HGU was required for weapons grade, which no Zone dare admit.

The nuclear fuel cycle produces a variety of materials at different processing steps, ranging from processed ore ("yellow cake") to uranium oxide fuel enriched in ^{235}U. Opportunities exist at many points during the fuel cycle for materials to be diverted outside the channels authorized for their legitimate manufacture, handling, and protection.

This Zonal veil of secrecy and non co-operation was one of the main reason Facilitators were formed, trained and authorised to police the world.

There is little point is trying to reason with an extremist that the salvation of the world is more important than their fanaticism.

Developing Signatures is a major focus of nuclear forensics as identifying signatures, which are the physical, chemical, and isotopic characteristics that distinguish one nuclear or radiological material from another. Signatures enable researchers to identify the processes used to initially create a material.

As early as 2030 Livermore scientists had developed validated signatures across the entire nuclear fuel cycle by experimental measurement and simulation.

Because nuclear material is transformed at different points during uranium concentration and enrichment processing, clues are unique to different stages.

Un-irradiated uranium reactor fuel pellets have inherent elemental oxygen content. Because the ratio of naturally occurring isotopes of oxygen-18 to oxygen-16 varies worldwide, these ratios correlate with the locations of production sites. The variations of lead isotopes provide clues about where a uranium compound was produced.

Age, colour, density, isotopic, trace elements, and surface characteristics of the uranium compound are important characteristics, including the effects of different uranium manufacturing processes on the grain size and microstructure of the finished product.

There exists a library of nuclear materials of known origin from around the world for comparing a sample's signature against known signatures from uranium mines and fabrication plants. Traceability should be incontrovertible and yet the ^{235}U materiel seized in the eight Zones has absolutely no history since used in the Egyptian power stations. When locally stored, this materiel was low grade.

What was adding to the frustrations was the expected signatures from the library of nuclear materials did not match the unique signature of the seized ^{235}U

It had been upgraded by a facility that provided absolutely no evidence of source.

This was making a mockery of the controls established by USA and Russian premiers Bush and Putin with the formation of the Global Nuclear Energy Partnership.

GNEP.

Established to deploy new technologies to recycle nuclear fuel, minimize waste, and improve the ability to keep nuclear technologies and materials out of the hands of terrorists.

GNEP had built recycling technologies that enhance energy security in a safe and environmentally responsible manner. GNEP was set up to make it impossible to divert nuclear materials or modify systems without immediate detection. The quintessential controls came from the material signature and incorporating tags into nuclear materials at different stages of the fuel cycle, so that the materials could be tracked and traced.

So how the bloody hell did this ^{235}U come to pass.

The questions outnumbered the answers drastically and both Facilitators were receiving daily demands for more information. This was made worse by the increasing threat of sending out more experienced Facilitators from both Zones, unless answers were forthcoming.

USA and Russia Zones being the most insistent.

The China Zone became belligerent, threatening direct intervention if Monique and Aaheru continued their apparent prevarication.

Aaheru continued his relentless pursuance of the daily processes including refuelling and maintenance outages occurring in containment, these involve:-

- Disassembly of the ventilation to the reactor vessel head area (Control Rod Drive Mechanisms)

- Removal and storage of the Pressuriser and Reactor Vessel Missile Shields, Reactor Vessel Head, Upper Internals of the reactor.

- Removal of spent fuel assemblies, addition of new fuel assemblies, shuffle of selected fuel assemblies to optimize the power profile over the cycle.

Another problem had been reported of structural faults in the containment chambers of the eight nuclear power plants that had received the illegal ^{235}U material. Examination revealed welding degradation and iron based corrosion, where stainless steels could not be used and substantial cracks in the concrete containment.

These nuclear power plants had been built on sites that were geologically extremely sound.

Any subterranean movement would be immediately detected by seismographs located every one hundred metres around each plant. Seismographs were also located progressively at two kilometres out for a distance of twenty kilometres.

The concrete structures had strain gauges built in to detect any movement at every square metre. Temperature, humidity, damp, sound, vibration and electromagnetic radiation sensors populated every building on the plant. Measurements were continuous with data recorders that read out locally with audio/visual alarming systems, with backup data streams to in-country Ministry Security facilities.

This level of control was mandatory for every nuclear power plant since 2020. Again the roles of the Facilitators required they had complete autonomy and unquestionable authority, to ensure these requirements and protocols were never breached.

Two weeks into their investigation they had no answers or even theories for their masters.

Chapter 3.
Follow the trail.

Zone 108 could no longer provide any further information or speculative theories and so Monique and Aaheru had no choice but to travel to the other eight Zones where the ^{235}U had been seized. These are

India	093
Bangladesh	076
Philippines	059
Vietnam	128
Sri Lanka	111
Nigeria.	067
Pakistan.	132
Indonesia.	099

,for each had reported intercepting significance quantities of enriched uranium all with the same batch traceability code. All had come from the Egyptian plant, over a period of six months, all now weapons grade enriched uranium.

They started in Zone 132, Pakistan, where they were joined by Dhul Fiqaar and Parveen, two local Facilitators who have specialised knowledge of nuclear physics and associated logistics. That know-how surely must provide added impetus to this prolonged investigation.

Alas it did not. The same questions, exactly the same findings, with a total lack of clarity.

Having four Facilitators on one case, albeit multi national will have one of only two outcomes. Total disharmony and confrontation or brainstorming options and solution proposals of the highest order.

Thankfully it was the latter, as Dhul Fiqaar casually commented over an evening meal, that they had not investigated the precise situation that led to the seizure of the significant amounts of ^{235}U It was an important development, that nobody had considered.

Next day all four travelled to the Ministry Security Division to pursue this question. The reply was astounding.

The duty officer had started his evening rota, when a signal flashed on his monitor stating, "Urgent message : dangerous consignment located in store TX-007-M."

To everyone's amazement, security and engineering found a one metre steel tube, containing one and half kilograms of enriched uranium in two and one half centimetre long, eighteen milli meter diameter pellets, arranged into long rods, collected into bundles.

Authentication was confirmed using a HPGe-based Radioisotope Identifier, also there was professional transportation packaging. So experts must have been involved in getting this ^{235}U to this place.

Located in a steel frame the external status-warning instruments flashing the contents signature code.

Knowledge that this material being supercritical and therefore would generate intense heat that would lead to a meltdown, just was not evident. The surface temperature was confirmed as below 100° C.

How could this be, a contradiction in basic physics. Understandably Security had quickly arranged for the material to be housed in a cooling pool.

Calls to the other Zones to establish how the ^{235}U was seized by the Zone Security divisions, returned similar circumstances. Slight differences in that the material was discovered inside secure storage areas, to the material arriving in vehicles again from a military warehouse that was had not been designed to house nuclear material.

There were no reported security operations, monitoring of suspect terrorists, uranium theft or loss. The sudden appearance of this material was simply notified to the authorities. It appeared from nowhere in similar quantities, in identical containers.

A meeting had been called for senior politicians from all Zones to attend in Beijing.

The Americans wanted New York, the Russians Moscow. Australia in Melbourne and the UK in London. The wrangling continued for a few days. Finally Beijing it was.

The four Facilitators were commanded to attend and to have a full story of what was going on regarding the mysterious appearance of the ^{235}U.

The meeting was set for two weeks time.

There absolutely has to be a very clever conspiracy.

But how was it possible to safely package and transport lethal ^{235}U, completely undetected, to eight separate Zones, all within days of each. It was logistically impossible, a nightmare, argued Dhul Fiqaar and Parveen, and yet, clearly it had been done.

There was no choice now other than to complete a full security audit at the source power station and the eight recipients of the ^{235}U material.

It was decided to change the working partnerships to Dhul Fiqaar and Monique, Parveen and Aaheru. The skills were not transferable but the working relationships might produce a different outlook and attitude to their investigations.

If these devices were being operated by some sinister organisation then their methods must be detectable. Transportation, activation and control must involve many co-ordinated, covert people.

Dhul Fiqaar and Monique returned to al-Dabaa, in Zone 108, with Parveen and Aaheru concentrating on the power plant in Karachi.

There followed a seemingly endless round of taped interviews, however each interviewee was required to be monitored with a lie detector. The idea of this being an option, was soon dispelled.

If an individual's honesty was questionable they would be required to undergo truth serums. Russian developed SP-117, Sodium Pentothal or quinuclidinyl benzilate. The choice was based on the individual being interrogated, with the emphasis on speed of response.

Protracted question and answer techniques on the grounds of civil liberties and human rights had long since been abandoned. The Facilitators had the awesome power to seek the truth at any cost, using any method. They were quite literally above any law, Zonal or global, excepting their respective Ministries.

A detailed walk through of all operations at the power plant gave no cause for concern. Even using comparative statement techniques, all answers agreed with documented records of procedural controls and materials compliance, all very evident.

Even employing intimidatory techniques failed to identify concerns. Sure people were extremely nervous and Monique in particular wasted no time in her very persuasive manner, to entice people to become overly relaxed, using double back questioning; still nothing.

The Facilitators reasoned that because of the proliferation of population control, using mind altering techniques, it was possible some, if not all, of the power plant staff had been brain washed or indoctrinated. With conditioned reflexes and programmed responses.

Unbeknown to those being interrogated, a signal generator was in use at Theta 4Hz - 8Hz frequency, to help induce a mind state, making it almost incapable of direct self control.

The 'raison d'être' was that if the individual had no reason to lie and that their defence mechanisms were suppressed, that mistakes would be made if they lied, or in any way attempted to distort the truth.

Their ability to be manipulative now reduced, thus encouraging intuitive openness i.e. the truth.

The final tool Monique employed was simply that of sitting in front of each person whilst interrogating and to fix a stare, sometimes even holding their hands. As an interrogator she really was unparalleled and normally very effective.

Nevertheless and despite this talent, Monique could not uncover any lie, or attempted deceit.

In a final, desperate move, both Monique and Dhul Fiqaar starting impromptu call back of individuals and asking exactly the same questions, in exactly the same order, to record and compare their answers and physiological responses. Again, absolutely nothing.

Close to despair, they returned each evening to their hotel, avoiding each other during dinner, choosing to have isolation both for relaxation and inevitably, further analytical thinking.

It was on the Thursday morning at breakfast, that a eureka moment again, this time for Dhul Fiqaar.

They had missed the most obvious fact, which was that everyone agreed with their peer groups when questioned about their movement, activities and disciplines.

The management team, the physicists, the engineers, the safety monitoring teams, security, catering, plant and domestic services, transport, finance. Quite literally there was not only a closeness in their answers but a precision. Their answers had a sequence, a pattern and consistency. So had they all been brainwashed ?

At last a possible breakthrough, but only a theory, speculative, nothing objective they could take to their Zonal Ministry masters, yet !

They invited Praveen and Aaheru to join them in al-Dabaa,. There was once again a very formidable team to unravel this mystery. This time with a focus.

Continuing interrogations was fruitless, for the plant personnel were now indifferent, no longer overawed.

Adjacent to every secure door throughout the nuclear power plant was an access panel with a DNA analyses pad that would illuminate and command the individual to provide a saliva sample.

This operation was then video recorded and the triple security check processed.

Another check involved a very sensitive weighing platform, accurate to within ten grams. Each staff member entering a secure location was required to stand on these scales on entry and exit, again using their security card and a unique numeric PIN pass code.

This quadruple check had never failed or malfunctioned. With these findings they concluded that only authorised staff were entering plant secure areas and that no theft was occurring.

Time was running out before the summit meeting in Beijing. They had to report daily but were extremely reluctant to admit their lack of progress. Lots of action but no results would not be well received by their Ministries who were now preparing their questions, concerns, denials and requirements. Potentially this summit could cause major consternation, especially amongst the one-time super powers.

There was absolutely no trust between the Zones, which would be further compounded if the highly regarded Facilitators were seen to appear clueless.

Doubts regarding the Facilitators would almost certainly follow and these were the last bastion. The only group of people above reproach, at least to date.

Tensions were rising, brinkmanship resuming, veiled threats uttered.

Daily feedback reporting had long since dispensed with niceties as their Ministries demanded answers and results. In fact these events were becoming so confrontational that the Facilitators would oft times lie about their availability, rather than make the call.

Sleepless nights soon became insomnia with Parveen, Aaheru, Monique and Dhul Fiqaar bickering about each others commitment and work rate. This disharmony even spilled into the investigation sessions they were holding at the al-Dabaa plant.

Such scenes really upset and worried plant personnel for the spectacle of Facilitators, the most powerful group of people on the planet, arguing and in conflict, led to fear and dread.

With only four days until the Beijing summit they decided to take time out from their fruitless investigations. To seek solace and privacy. To collect their thoughts away from the tensions and aggravations each were experiencing.

Monique decided to escape to Alexandria, and though this was a nightmare for her security guards, her insistence resulted in a 36 hour departure from the al-Dabaa plant and much needed time to relax. This proved very naïve on reflection.

Most of the one-time luxury hotels were dilapidated and quite frankly, uninhabitable. However and as always, because of her status, she was found a coastline retreat, that gave her the escape she so badly needed.

Unpacked, dined, a hot bath and a glass of agreeable wine found Monique sprawled, semi naked on her bed, with thoughts of her London apartment.

How had she described it:- uninspiring, dispassionate and empty. At least there was a hint of normality there, without this endless pressure.

Though she also reminded herself of her thoughts then:-

"Epargnez-moi cette vie que j'ai choisie"

Guess there's no simple answer then, she mused. Just have to get on with it.

Small talk with other guests, passed most of the evening and the long awaited amble to her room, with a dismissive but appreciative wave to her bodyguards.

Into the room, clothes off and into bed. I have tomorrow she thought but then back to the enigma and her co Facilitators who hopefully have been inspired on the next course of action.

Sleep came reluctantly and was short lived as she floated between dreams and stark, disturbing reality.

Time and again she woke up with a start. For fucks sake she cursed. I am tired, so bloody tired. Is it so much to ask for a good nights sleep.

The room window was slightly open and the arid night air whispered, gushed, sighed and purred a tantalizing lullaby. Then it happened, not suddenly but assuredly.

The Presence could not be seen, heard, touched or smelled but as certain as day follows night, it was there in the room, with her.

Her mental state varied from uncertainty to abject fear and yet strangely she did not feel threatened or in real danger. She choked herself back from calling out for her bodyguards. Her personal attack alarm that was GPS linked, trembled in her hand.

Though the Global Positioning Systems had been switched off for the vast majority of its functions, certain systems and accesses however had been left open. The Facilitators were covered at all times, as their movements were GPS monitored to within one metre.

But what would she say if she summoned help. It would seem liked she had lost her senses and become deranged. Christ! that would be all that was needed to have her recalled home for a complete re-evaluation with the possibility of her becoming just another citizen.

Or even institutionalised after a mind clearing programme, for she knew so much, to roam freely.

Her thoughts were now in turmoil and she trembled helplessly.

The omnipresence was still there, she just knew it. But where is it, what is it, is it an imaginative stress related breakdown. She closed her eyes, took several deep breaths and tried desperately to relax.

She remembered no more. Almost as if she had been sedated until the gentle purring of the wake up system, unlike hers at home, urged her to abandon sleep.

Her authority was immediately challenged, as she called out for the shower and music to commence. Silly girl she cursed and revoked such absent minded folly. No voice controlled systems in this hotel.

The experience would not leave her and even in the dinning room, over breakfast she had the inexplicable sensation of the Presence again.

She found herself staring around the restaurant, looking suspiciously at fellow diners and staff as if they would yield some form of explanation.

Nothing was making sense and she was becoming more aggravated as she played with her food and sipped at her coffee.

"Everything okay"?, questioned one of her bodyguards, which brought a sigh of distain, followed by a look that would melt an iceberg.

She spent most of the morning wandering along the shoreline. The beaches, sand and rippling sea felt indeed therapeutic but still she felt the Presence.

Exercise your intellect she challenged herself. If this Presence really exists, then am I open to contact or am I blocking contact, by close-mindedness.

Reach out for it, she contemplated, but how, Not through speech or gesture for sure. She sat on an aged, weather beaten beach boulder and allowed the sun to embrace her face and the gentle breeze to wash over her body.

She could feel it working, her trepidation slowly abating and her tension turning to curiosity.

Slowly she started sequencing the events that brought her to this point in time. It became apparent that how the ^{235}U came into existence, was not important. It was why this inexplicable chain of events had occurred. Lateral thinking, not vertical paranoia was needed. Composure and logic, not emotive, knee jerk overload.

The disciplined, logical and pragmatic Monique was slowly returning.

The return journey to al-Dabaa passed quickly, as she concentrated on the sequence of events, scribbling notes and diagrams onto her electronic, encrypted notepad.

It was 7pm when she arrived back in the hotel. Overnight bag back into her room and then joined Parveen, Aaheru, and Dhul Fiqaar at the bar, for pre evening meal drinks. It felt good being back with them.

Niceties exchanged, they ordered their meals and small talked about the obvious. Main concern was the upcoming Beijing summit and what they should say to their respective Ministries. Individual reports, or a joint communiqué.

The latter could result in condemnation of them all if there was rejection of their investigation findings thus far. But, if they reported individually, then criticism of not sharing their resources for the common good. Talk about a Catch 22 situation. They are Facilitators not bloody politicians, they protested to each other.

Dining finished around 9:30pm and then an agreement to retire for the day and retreat to their bedrooms. Meet at breakfast and then back to the plant.

No surprise when all four, Parveen, Aaheru, Monique and Dhul Fiqaar appeared one at a time back at the bar. Unable to sleep or even relax, they needed some liquid refreshment to help, preferably about 40% proof.

A couple of inebriating rounds and tensions started easing with Parveen the first to speak, the unspeakable.

As she described her experience during the last twenty four hours, the countenance on the other faces quickly changed.

She had first sensed the Presence during her midday shower, for she had returned from the plant at 11am, totally frustrated and with Monique away, a feeling of isolation and helplessness. No reflection on the guys, she just needed another female.

The afternoon brought no relief to her as a dread had taken over. She had even asked one of her bodyguards to thoroughly check her room for surveillance devices. Nothing found. Not really surprising she thought.

Aaheru and Dhul Fiqaar then relayed what had happened to them, all the time trying to sound macho and analytical, but their recollections sounded trite.

Nevertheless the disconcerting fact was that all four Facilitators had a similar experience. Each had frozen, been totally confused and bewildered and then fought to regain their composure. A very unnerving time, that all really wanted to deny, but couldn't.

Each had initially decided not to share their experience, fearing ridicule or rebuffal. And yet each is a Facilitator. Highly educated and trained with personal and professional qualities, few possess.

They are quite simply amongst the elite of all Zones.

However if they have any self doubt or loose their investigative abilities, then they must be decommissioned. This, a real fear they have, and serves to undermine their full potential in this investigation.

It also raises the fundamental question of who polices the police. This falls to their masters in the Ministries of Security in each Zone. And so the love-hate relationship tensions continue.

Again, distracting thoughts. They have a job of work to do and these eerie developments serve only to confuse the issue, compounded by the demands for answers, to this imponderable quandary.

Parveen suggested they retire and document their thoughts on how to proceed. Two hours were allotted for a secret meet at midday to decide the next steps.

Surveillance was stepped up by the eight bodyguards and a secure room found for the Facilitators to use. The hotel management and guests became increasingly curious at the behaviour of the Facilitators. Some knew who they were, most were indifferent. Just curious.

No-one had any idea of what was going on but as an added precaution it was decided to commandeer a secure office at the plant, starting tomorrow, for all deliberations.

Also their documents and mobile media systems, anything but personal clothing from now on, had to be left at the plant.

They also decided on a collective status report to their Ministries. It read:-

"As a direct result of our investigations, we can report that nuclear fuel disciplines have not been breached or compromised and that the toxic and lethal materials are now securely quarantined. That no danger therefore exists to any Zone and there is no global threat.

Hazard containment has been our priority, as we now concentrated on how this occurred."

Thought we weren't politicians chuckled Dhul Fiqaar, as they gathered again to decide their next move.

They decided to investigate how the message appeared on the monitor of the duty security officer at the Pakistan plant. Using play back they reviewed the message:-

"Urgent message : dangerous consignment located in store TX-007-M."

The technologists responsible for electronic data processing, storage and transfer, traced back through every server on the plant.

That message had no I.P. address reference. It had apparently appeared out of the ether. No explanation could be offered.

Likewise when they investigated how the ^{235}U materialised at the other eight locations. No manner of questioning or back tracking could provide an explanation.

Over dinner Monique and Dhul Fiqaar commented that neither had felt the Presence that day and yet they could not entertain the idea that it had left. A stand off, maybe.

Parveen and Aaheru agreed but despite the mutual acceptance of relief, the atmosphere over breakfast was discernibly different. More relaxed.

None of them had slept well but more disturbingly, each had dreamt of a nuclear bomb attack on an unspecified city and a full retaliation, leading to global destruction. That's no dream, but a bloody nightmare.

Clearly the images they had experienced had a profound effect on them, as they sat in complete silence on the way back to the plant.

Once again they felt absolutely helpless and such was their loss of personal and collective confidence, they decided to examine the ^{235}U found in TX-007-M.

They gowned up, attached radioactive detectors and entered the secure air locked doors to the delivery room from where all ^{235}U was transferred on the way to the nuclear reactor core.

The storage engineers lifted the viewing shields and operated the control buttons to start the conveyor belt. The stainless steel, lead lined doors slid open and the belt began to move. Warning sirens and lights commenced and the positive airflow rushed through.

Seconds passed with the belt empty. The engineers stopped the belt and restarted the sequence. More seconds passed. Uneasiness rippled across everyone. So where the bloody hell is it, demanded Dhul Fiqaar ?

The engineers activated the transport line internal cameras that lead back to the ^{235}U storage racks. In fact all uranium, irrespective of grade, has exactly the same control for storage, monitoring and retrieval system.

All material was present, except the unaccountable ^{235}U

It had gone. !!

Near panic pervaded the Facilitators and all those present. This really cannot be happening !

Chapter 4.
The Beijing summit.

Delegates arrived progressively, over a three day period.

Normally at these summits or conventions, each attendee would have a parallel, private agenda that would take in golf, sight seeing and socialising.

Human nature normally transcends formal commitment. Not this time, for the stony, expressionless face of each delegate underlined the absolute seriousness and concerns each Zone representative held.

The ludicrously tense situation was further exacerbated by the refusal to share the reports sent by the Facilitators. So three Zones with their reports and 144 without. This was taking brinkmanship and secrecy to extremes and was surely folly.

The Chairman and Host, opened the summit with a statement, wasting no time on welcoming sentiments or wishes of good will:-

"We are gathered here quite simply because highly enriched uranium ^{235}U has been intercepted by security Ministries in eight Zones. It must follow that forces not known to us all, are at work, to make nuclear devices for purposes of mass destruction.

It is in the interests of all 147 Zones to identify the source of the uranium and eradicate those responsible for its obtainment, transport and eventual application, as a matter of extreme urgency. In a world torn apart by distrust, egoism and parochial agendas we must unite, to resolve this issue", he concluded.

Each delegate stared eagerly at their monitor. The technology meant that as the host spoke each monitor would be configured to translate and display precisely what was said in every language known in the Zones. The delegates would interpret the sincerity, or lack of, from the host's voice and body language.

It had long been accepted that individuals not being truthful would betray themselves through speech as opposed to facial expressions or body language.

It is argued that for sedation to be of any use, the quantity required would directly impair the vocal range for speed, volume and intonation. So the voice remains a truth organ, something that should be trusted.

But at this stage the Delegates were being spoken to, not questioned and each already knew of the illegal ^{235}U being simultaneously present in eight Zones.

It was agreed that Zones would be grouped to brainstorm ideas and solutions. But with four top Facilitators already working at source, most Delegates really felt quite helpless, with unfounded speculation being all they could muster.

It should also be pointed out that at this time the, delegates did not know the ^{235}U from the al-Dabaa plant was missing.

All hell would let loose when they did.

Parveen, Aaheru, Monique and Dhul Fiqaar had confirmed to their horror that the other eight batches of ^{235}U had also gone missing. And it was established all within a six hour period. None of the storage areas had been accessed, without the direct authorisation of the Facilitators, which of course had never been given.

So how did this stuff get out, how was it transported, by whom, to where and for what.

This had become a bloody cat and mouse game on a horrific scale. All nuclear power plants had been alerted to be diligent when monitoring, for material movement. If it went missing, changed locations, increased or decreased in quantity, or just appeared.

Each Zone Ministry of Defence were likewise informed to increase policing of their nuclear weapon stockpiles and all delivery systems.

Christ! uranium is used in so many applications; so where to limit these notifications. It was decided only where there is, or could be, weapons grade uranium.

These seemingly unfathomable questions just turned all logic on its head and almost as a place of retreat, the Facilitators returned to the question of the Presence.

As nothing had been seen, heard, touched or smelled, then just what had they all experienced? Man's pre-occupation with extra terrestrials had been based upon the human form and characteristics which had been discounted since the early 19th century.

Stories from delusional sightings by oft times backwoods communities, right through to alleged scientific data gathering, following reports from various military and commercial pilots.

These early and unsubstantiated reports dealt only with space vehicle sightings, not extra terrestrial life forms.

Nothing stacked up. Scientific, factual evidence did not exist, just speculation on the probability of not just humans populating a planet in the Earth's solar system.

Space probes and limited space exploration by man ended in 2038 when a manned mission to Mars completely failed with total loss of the spacecraft and crew. This caused such consternation that the USA, China and Russia agreed a treaty of close-earth research only, with a massive space station, to house a mixed race, sex and age generation of astronauts.

The Global Harmony space station was totally self sufficient with a near earth orbit of 350 km altitude, average speed of 28,000 km/h, completing 16 orbits per day. Could this now be the base for the Presence visiting the earth or having incredible remote powers of influence. Anyway, the Facilitators understood this space station was unmanned since Zonalisation.

However, into this background the preconceived human idea of what would constitute an extra terrestrial life form would need to be considered.

Entertaining such a concept would negate any influence the Presence would have with human parameters, systems of expectations and conditioned reflexes.

The motivation or justification for any interference by the Presence are erroneous human concepts of greed, survival, revenge and ambition, all of which may be erroneous. But then again if survival, was it for the world's population benefit, or for the Presence.

Next the Facilitators turned their attention to the question of making a nuclear bomb. Just what was involved. By knowing this maybe they could anticipate what might happen next, and take proactive action.

Back to basics seemed indulgent and time wasting when they are already working against the clock with their masters locked in limbo in Beijing. But they must make a stand, to fully focus on at least one aspect of the evolving nightmare.

Aaheru made the necessary hurried arrangements for the Facilitators to visit a local munitions factory, directly involved in the manufacture of thermal nuclear bombs. So what is involved.

Firstly a preamble:-

Nuclear Weapons, explosive devices, designed to release nuclear energy on a large scale, are used primarily in military applications. The first atomic bomb, which was tested July 16, 1945, at Alamogordo, New Mexico, represented a completely new type of artificial explosive. All explosives prior to that time derived their power from the rapid burning or decomposition of some chemical compound. Such chemical processes release only the energy of the outermost electrons in the atom.

Nuclear explosives involve energy sources within the core, or nucleus, of the atom.

The atomic bomb gained its power from the splitting, or fission, of all the atomic nuclei in several kilograms of plutonium. A ball sized sphere produced explosion equal to 20.Kilo tons of TNT.

The A-bomb was developed, constructed, and tested by the USA Manhattan Project, 1942.

Post WW11 the U.S. Atomic Energy Commission became responsible for the oversight of all nuclear matters, including weapons research. Other types of bombs were developed to tap the energy of light elements, such as hydrogen. In these bombs the source of energy is the fusion process, in which nuclei of the isotopes [*each of two or more forms of a chemical element with the same atomic number but different numbers of neutrons*] of hydrogen combine to form a heavier helium nucleus.

Fission Weapons

In 1905 Albert Einstein published his special theory of relativity. According to this theory, the relation between mass and energy is expressed by the equation $E = MC^2$, which states that a given mass (m) is associated with an amount of energy (E) equal to this mass multiplied by the square of the speed of light (c). A very small amount of matter is equivalent to a vast amount of energy. For example, 1 kg (2.2 lb) of matter converted completely into energy would be equivalent to the energy released by exploding 22 megatons of TNT.

In 1939, by the German chemists Otto Hahn and Fritz Strassmann (1902-80), who split the uranium atom into two roughly equal parts by bombardment with neutrons. The Austrian physicist Lise Meitner, and British physicist Otto Robert Frisch (1904-79), explained the process of nuclear fission, which placed the release of atomic energy within reach.

The Chain Reaction

When the uranium or other suitable nucleus fissions, it breaks up into a pair of nuclear fragments and releases energy.

At the same time, the nucleus emits very quickly a number of fast neutrons, the same type of particle that initiated the fission of the uranium nucleus.

This makes it possible to achieve a self-sustaining series of nuclear fissions; the neutrons that are emitted in fission produce a chain reaction, with continuous release of energy.

Nuclear Fission and Nuclear Fusion

Both nuclear fission and nuclear fusion reactions can be used to generate large amounts of energy for destructive purposes. When an atom of 235U is bombarded by a neutron, it splits into atoms of cesium and rubidium, releasing a large amount of energy and three additional neutrons. These neutrons, if not controlled, can then cause more 235U atoms to split, leading rapidly to a nuclear explosion (A-bomb).

Fusion reactions release energy when two light nuclei combine to make a heavier atom.

Starting with why Nuclear Fission bombs use uranium-235 as fuel. Uranium is the heaviest naturally occurring element on Earth, and it has two isotopes - uranium-238 and uranium-235, both of which are barely stable. Both isotopes also have an unusually large number of neutrons. Although ordinary uranium will always have 92 protons, U-238 has 146 neutrons, while U-235 has 143 neutrons.

Both isotopes of uranium are radioactive, and they eventually decay over time. 235U, however, has an extra property that makes it useful for both nuclear-power production and nuclear-bomb production.

235U is one of the few materials that can undergo induced fission.

Instead of waiting more than 700 million years for uranium to naturally decay, the element can be broken down much faster if a neutron runs into a 235U nucleus. The nucleus will absorb the neutron without hesitation, become unstable and split immediately.

In a fission bomb, the fuel must be kept in separate subcritical masses, which will not support fission, to prevent premature detonation.

Critical mass is the minimum mass of fissionable material required to sustain a nuclear fission reaction.

The two or more subcritical masses must be brought together to form a supercritical mass, which will provide more than enough neutrons to sustain a fission reaction at the time of detonation.

Free neutrons must be introduced into the supercritical mass to start the fission and as much of the material as possible must be fissioned before the bomb explodes, to prevent fizzle.

To bring the subcritical masses together into a supercritical mass, two techniques are used:

Implosion or Gun-Triggered.

Implosion: Neutrons are introduced by making a neutron generator. This generator is a small pellet of polonium and beryllium, separated by foil within the fissionable fuel core. In this generator: The foil is broken when the subcritical masses come together and polonium spontaneously emits alpha particles. These alpha particles then collide with beryllium-9 to produce beryllium-8 and free neutrons. The neutrons then initiate fission.

Finally, the fission reaction is confined within a dense material called a tamper, which is usually made of uranium-238. The tamper gets heated and expanded by the fission core. This expansion of the tamper exerts pressure back on the fission core and slows the core's expansion. The tamper also reflects neutrons back into the fission core, increasing the efficiency of the fission reaction.

In an implosion-triggered design, the explosives fire, creating a shock wave. The shock wave propels the plutonium pieces together into a sphere.

The plutonium pieces strike a pellet of beryllium/polonium at the centre, fission reaction begins. The bomb explodes

Gun-triggered Fission bomb. The simplest way to bring the subcritical masses together is to make a gun that fires one mass into the other.

A sphere of U-235 is made around the neutron generator and a small bullet of U-235 is removed.

The bullet is placed at the one end of a long tube with explosives behind it, while the sphere is placed at the other end. The explosives fire and propel the bullet down the barrel. The bullet strikes the sphere and generator, initiating the fission reaction. The bomb explodes.

Having exhausted this review of how nuclear bombs are designed and function, had not really advanced their thinking, except to know what facility and resources would be required to make a bomb.

With sufficient safeguards for heat and radiation, any proficient engineer could produce a nuclear explosive device anywhere in the world, in any Zone.

Monique could feel herself wanting to scream, as she pushed her way past Aaheru , Dhul Fiqaar and Parveen to escape the room and find fresh air.

It was 10pm, she was hungry and it was really cold but emotion had taken over and she could actually feel tears well up in her tired and exhausted eyes.

That tingling sensation again, oh no, the Presence had returned. Christ ! its here she heard herself whisper, as she spun around, looking for it.

Just one word echoed and echoed in her turmoil. Why, why, why ??? over and again.

Why what ? What the fuck does that mean she cursed.

Speak to me, she demanded, communicate, for goodness sake, stop playing this bloody infantile game.

We are all desperate with our leaders gathered at a Summit that could lead to hostilities, even a world wide nuclear war.

Is this what you want, are you instrumental in what is happening. Do you even exist, or am I and my colleagues going crazy, she shouted. Silence followed.

Nothing, absolutely nothing. Not even the sounds of her own thoughts or an echo of her emotional shouting.

She broke down in a flood of tears and soon felt the assuring arms of Parveen, and Dhul Fiqaar around her.

Come on Monique, this is tearing us all apart.

Though Monique was in no state of mind to assume full rational thought, she was wrestling with how the Presence was getting to her, when all physical attributes simply did not apply.

Could it be possible that the Presence was communicating subliminally, maybe at the Theta wave range of 4-7 HZ. It is understood Theta is one of the more elusive and extraordinary realms and is also known as the twilight state, where people normally only experience fleetingly, as they rise up out of the depths of delta upon waking, or drifting off to sleep.

In Theta they are in a waking-dream, vivid imagery flashes before the mind's eye and they are receptive to information beyond the normal conscious awareness.

It also awakens intuition and other extrasensory perception skills.

She returned to the hotel. A light supper and to bed. No rest again, as the Presence returned and the haunting taunt of why ? this was becoming a fixation, that blocked out all other rational thought.

Breakfast was missed, just coffee and biscuits at the plant.

More unreasonable demands from their masters in Beijing. Tensions were such that the Facilitators were stopping each other from responding with obscenities and threats of resignations.

Back at the Summit, belligerence had started, with the former super powers wanting to send in specialist teams to the eight Zones where the illegal ^{235}U had been found.

Outrage and anger with many of the Delegates protesting, "Why the hell have we all agreed to the Facilitators having such powers of search and authority to act, without constraint or question." But to dismantle the whole global system of Facilitation would indeed be a retrograde step, that would lead to anarchy. And everyone there knew it.

Then the Summit was told that the eight illegal ^{235}U packages were misplaced. Could not be found or traced.

The response was predictably extreme disbelief, anger and suspicion. Hardly surprising, considering the distrusting state the world had been in for so long.

Negotiations, compromise, reason, understanding, forgiveness. All forgotten concepts now.

Many Delegates stormed out of the Summit hall when told and just drove around Beijing not knowing what to do next. Paranoia pulling their thoughts in every direction.

Some wanted to return home, even went to the airports, sat in the departure lounges and then hurried back to the Summit hall. They were like headless chickens, incapable of controlled logic and reason.

Each delegate had their own team of academics, philosophers, mathematicians, scientists, psychologists, historians, diplomats and personal advisors, who doubled up as translators, for those, off-the-record, chats.

These support teams were absolutely impotent.

Not one on them had a clue of what next to do. Everyone was feeling completely useless, the Delegates, their teams and most alarmingly, the Facilitators.

It soon became evident that some Zones were in collusion and had started considered discussions of clandestine coalitions. All completely off the record and yet nearly every Delegate started considering their potentially closest ally on many fronts. Economic, political, military alignments. That occupied more of the Delegates time than formal assessment and decision making, on the actual problem.

Both First strike and retaliatory strategies were being seriously considered. Though this was not communicated to their own Zone Ministries and definitely not the stranded and isolated Facilitators. Parveen, Aaheru, Monique and Dhul Fiqaar had already been assigned to the redundancy list, after they had been publicly condemned as failures.

Trying to understand what realistic fears the Delegates had, came to a head during one formal session, when Zone 135 from Chile tabled a motion of no confidence in the Summit.

When questioned why, he blurted out the many undercover meetings Delegates had been having and produced recorded evidence of such discussions between 004 the UK and 049 France. Absolute uproar as near hysteria set in. With Zone Delegate after Zone Delegate rounding on the two accused Delegates, who could offer no explanation. Acutely embarrassing.

The Summit Chairman realising how desperate the whole situation had become, proposed a cessation of the Summit for two weeks.

He made a proviso though. When all 147 Zones reconvened, each must bring a detailed strategy on how to neutralise the threat of the mysterious ^{235}U .

This seemingly pointless requirement was meant to distract the Delegates passion from hostilities and defence, over to problem solving and collaboration.

As the Delegates limousines rolled away and the airports transported the Delegates home, an atmosphere of confusion and apprehension settled over Beijing.

Word eventually reached the Facilitators and each read this as a respite, a chance to regroup, collect thoughts and concentrate of objectives.

Progressive thinking techniques had been implanted in their minds during training. For one does not become a Facilitator by simply applying basic logic.

The screening, interviewing, selection and training period, exceeds three years. Lateral thinking and reversed conjecture were just two weapons in their intellectual armoury.

Reason not force. Solution not problem. Outcome forecast scenarios. Contingency planning. Irrational intervention. Reverse social engineering. And religion, the most contentious of all.

There is an argument that too many options serve only to choke solutions. One can be too bright and knowledgeable for their, or anyone else's good.

Maybe, just maybe, these Facilitators were such people. Over qualified and too profound in their approach. Had common sense been forgotten, has the obvious not been seen or simply overlooked.

Even worse, has their apparent failure and emotional roller coaster, stripped them of real ability.

So they thought of the unthinkable. Passing the problem to a team of laypeople. Once accepted in principle, should these people be from the plant where at least some subject matter knowledge would exist or, should the people be totally removed from this environment.

Just taken from the local population at random.

This was an extremely risky strategy for the very nature of laypersons involvement would cause everyone to question why. Would they return to their communities and say not a single word.

Think not, commented Aaheru.

We could start something irreversible. And then what of the reputations of these so-called demigods, proven to be human and fallible after all.

Then if their masters found out, after the fiasco of the last three weeks, they would be finished. But what matters most argued Dhul Fiqaar, our pride and standing, or the solution to what could be a major nuclear confrontation, with possible global implications.

The four Facilitators were clearly divided on this question and agreed a 48 hour stay of execution, when an agreement must be reached.

Chapter 5.
On the brink of War.

It would be folly to think the Delegates had gone home to concentrate on problem solving of the illegal, mysterious ^{235}U.

Many of them convened War Cabinets within hours of arriving home. This met with immediate reaction from the Facilitators in their respective Zones, who were formed to ensure global peace and threat eradication, was maintained.

They never needed reminding that the Facilitators main purpose was to identify and neutralise threats to Zonal stability and therefore world peace.

However, long had gone the days when the bad guys wore black and the good guys, white. Beliefs, convictions, ideology, religion, historical dogma, basic needs for survival, traditions, technology, even mother nature herself, all contributed to a very complicated, contradictory and constantly changing world.

There had been three world wars. 1914 – 1918 : 1939 – 1945 : and finally 2018 - 2021, though the latter was concentrated mainly in the Middle East involving the Israeli and Palestinian nations, vying for the same areas of land.

Religious fervour and the previous persecution of the Jewish Race, had forged a country so strong and resolute that it would have readily committed the last Jew standing to extinction.

The status of this conflict to a world war was because of the backing these two warring nations had.

The Jews, had the might of the USA and the Palestinians, backed by many in the Arab World, who often talked of a Holy War 'Jihad'. These two nations had been engaged in cross border battles for many years, despite peace initiatives.

This conflict saw the deployment of nuclear weapons delivery systems from land and sea and the determination of all parties, not to acquiesce. The one factor that eventually brought an end to the terrors of a nuclear exchange was that some Arabs wanted Iran to be neutralised by the USA.

This was eventually achieved by the assassination of many of the Iranian ruling party, then civil insurrection, funded and promoted covertly by the USA. Not for the first or last time.

Lessons in history given to all Facilitators included detailed studies of different kinds of warfare. This was essential for them to be effective in their roles.

Asymmetric.   A military situation in which two belligerents of unequal strength interact and take advantage of their respective strengths and weaknesses. This interaction often involves strategies and tactics outside the bounds of conventional warfare, often referred to as terrorism.

Biological warfare   Also known as germ warfare, is the use of any organism (bacteria, virus or other disease-causing organism) or toxin found in nature, as a weapon of war. It is meant to incapacitate or kill an adversary. Also be defined as the employment of biological agents to produce casualties in man or animals and damage to plants or material; or defense against such employment.

Chemical warfare   Chemical warfare is warfare (associated military operations) using the toxic properties of chemical substances to kill, injure or incapacitate an enemy.

Electronic warfare   Electronic warfare refers to mainly non-violent practices used chiefly to support other areas of warfare. The term means to encompass the interception and decoding of enemy radio communications, and the communications technologies and cryptography methods used to counter such interception, as well as jamming, radio stealth and other related areas.

Over the latter years of the 20th century and early years of the 21st century this has expanded to cover a wide range of areas: the use of, detection of and avoidance of detection by Radar and Sonar systems, computer hacking and Space warfare etc.

Fourth generation warfare   (4GW) is a concept used to describe the decentralized nature of modern warfare. The simplest definition includes any war in which one of the major participants is not a state but rather a violent ideological network. Fourth Generation wars are characterized by a blurring of the lines between war and politics, soldier and civilian, conflict and peace, battlefield and safety.

While this term is similar to terrorism and asymmetric warfare, it is much narrower. Classical insurgencies and the Indian Wars are examples of Pre-Modern War, not 4GW. Fourth generation warfare usually has the insurgency group or non-state side trying to implement their own government or re-establish an old government over the one currently running the territory. The blurring of lines between state and non-state is further complicated in a democracy by the power of the media.

Land/ground warfare

Infantry.   in modern times would consist of Mechanized infantry and Airborne forces. Usually having a type of rifle or sub-machine gun, an infantryman is the basic unit of an army.

Armored warfare   in modern times involves a variety of Armored fighting vehicles for the purpose of battle and support. Tanks or other armored vehicles (such as armored personnel carriers or tank destroyers) are slower, yet stronger hunks of metal.

They are invulnerable to enemy machine gun fire but prone to rocket infantry, mines, and aircraft so are usually accompanied by infantry. Armored vehicles can play a critical role in urban combat.

Artillery   in contemporary times, is distinguished by its large calibre, firing an explosive shell or rocket, and being of such a size and weight as to require a specialized mount for firing and transport. Weapons covered by this term include "tube" artillery such as the howitzer, cannon, mortar, and field gun and "rocket" artillery. The term "artillery" has traditionally not been used for projectiles with internal guidance systems, even though some artillery units employ surface-to-surface missiles. Recent advances in terminal guidance systems for small munitions has allowed large calibre shells to be fitted with precision guidance fuses, blurring this distinction.

Guerrilla warfare   Guerrilla warfare is defined as fighting by groups of irregular troops (guerrillas) within areas occupied by the enemy. When guerrillas obey the laws of conventional warfare they are entitled, if captured, to be treated as ordinary prisoners of war; however, they are often executed by their captors. The tactics of guerrilla warfare stress deception and ambush, as opposed to mass confrontation, and succeed best in an irregular, rugged, terrain and with a sympathetic populace, whom guerrillas often seek to win over or dominate by propaganda, reform, and terrorism. Guerrilla warfare has played a significant role in modern history, especially when waged by Communist liberation movements in Southeast Asia (most notably in the Vietnam War) and elsewhere.

Guerrilla fighters gravitate toward weapons which are easily accessible, low in technology and low in cost. A typical arsenal of the modern guerrilla would include the AK-47, RPGs and Improvised explosive devices. The guerrilla doctrines' main disadvantage is the inability to access more advanced equipment due to economic, influence, and accessibility issues. They must rely on small unit tactics involving hit and run. This situation leads to low intensity warfare and asymmetrical warfare. The rules of Guerrilla warfare are to fight a little and then to retreat.

Intelligence Warfare.   Propaganda is an ancient form of disinformation concerted with sending a set of messages aimed at influencing the opinions or behavior of large numbers of people. Instead of impartially providing information, propaganda in its most basic sense presents information in order to influence its audience. The most effective propaganda is often completely truthful, but some propaganda presents facts selectively to encourage a particular synthesis, or gives loaded messages in order to produce an emotional rather than rational response to the information presented. The desired result is a change of the cognitive narrative of the subject in the target audience.

Psychological warfare had its beginnings during the campaigns of Genghis Khan through the allowance of certain civilians of the nations, cities, and villages to flee said place, spreading terror and fear to neighboring principalities. Psychological_actions have the primary purpose of influencing the opinions, emotions, attitudes, and behavior of hostile foreign groups in such a way as to support the achievement of national objectives.

Information warfare Made possible by the widespread use of the electronic media during the Second World War, Information warfare is a kind of warfare where information and attacks on information and its system are used as a tool of warfare. Some examples of this type of warfare are electronic "sniffers" which disrupt international fund-transfer networks as well as the signals of television and radio stations. Jamming such signals can allow participants in the war to use the stations for a misinformation campaign.

Naval warfare takes place on the high seas (blue water navy). Usually, only large, powerful nations have competent blue water or deep water navies. Modern navies primarily use aircraft carriers, submarines, frigates, cruisers, and destroyers for combat.

This provides a versatile array of attacks, capable of hitting ground targets, air targets, or other seafaring vessels. Most modern navies also have a large air support contingent, deployed from aircraft carriers.

Network-centric warfare is essentially a new military doctrine made possible by the Information Age. Weapons platforms, sensors and command and control centers are being connected through high-speed communication networks. The doctrine is related to the Revolution in Military Affairs debate. The overall network which enables this strategy in the United States military is called the Global Information Grid.

Nuclear war is a type of warfare which relies on nuclear weapons. There are two types of warfare in this category. In a limited nuclear war, a small number of weapons are used in a tactical exchange aimed primarily at opposing military forces. In a full-scale nuclear war, large numbers of weapons are used in an attack aimed at entire countries. This type of warfare would target both military bases and civilians.

Space warfare   is warfare that occurs outside the Earth's atmosphere. The weapons would include Orbital weaponry and Space weapons. High value outer space targets would include satellites and weapon platforms. Limited real weapons exist in space at this time, and ground-to-space missiles have been successfully tested against target satellites.

Future warfare   Future conflict will not be a precise science: it will remain an unpredictable activity. Adversaries state, state-proxies and non-state and threats. Conventional and unconventional will blur. The range of threats will spread, with increased proliferation of Weapons of Mass Destruction (WMD), cyberspace, and other novel and irregular threats. Even during wars of national survival or the destruction of WMD, conflict will remain focused on influencing people. The battle of the narratives will be key, and countries must conduct protracted influence activity, coordinated centrally and executed locally.

Maintaining public support will be essential for success on all operations. Critical to this will be legitimacy and effective levels of force protection. Qualitative advantage may no longer be assumed in the future. Some adversaries may be able to procure adequate quality as well as afford greater quantity, whereas we will be unable to mass sufficient quality or quantity everywhere that it is needed.

This ambivalence was being seen in Zone after Zone, for the Facilitators had become totally accepted as independent peace keepers. Override them now and what hope would the world have in future, if this one problem resulted in their disbandment. No, no, this must not be allowed to happen, came the call from many senior people in every Zone.

There was already near dictatorship politics in most Zones but this was engineered to keep the masses in check, not to turn against the very hierarchy who controlled each Zone.

Thing is, the Facilitators have this awesome power to go anywhere, ask any question and not be challenged.

But that authority was only ever intended for work outside of their indigenous Zone. Not within, which is now how it was being applied.

This domino effect leading from the first discovery of the illegal ^{235}U in Pakistan was startling. The world was being pushed to the brink of a global war and yet the safeguard mechanisms that man had devised, seemed to be keeping the tensions in check. At least for now.

What forces are at work creating this situation. Is there an alien intervention somehow orchestrating the thoughts and actions of so many people, in so many Zones.

The stability was precarious at best, especially when considering those nations who were always seen as volatile with extreme religious beliefs having reverted to uncompromising fundamentalism.

It could only be hoped that the Facilitators could hold their leaders back from irrational behaviour.

Deterrence Theory was as true now as when first accepted, and is a sobering realisation.

But if a Zone had continued to experience deprivation, natural disasters, social disintegration, violence, corruption and abuse from its political leaders, then what care that Zone.

Maybe Armageddon is the only answer to purge this vile planet of the impurities brought about by mankind, the most ambivalent creature ever born, torn between greed and caring. There is no middle ground.

It would be a Zone like this that would start a war. Limited to start with, depending on their nuclear capability and delivery systems plus the defence capabilities of the Zone where the nuclear devices were aimed. The Arab States had often talked of a Jihad, Holy War, with all kindred Zones being involved.

And then what of Zones who had secretly developed nuclear capabilities. They could only test these devices in underground facilities which would surely be detected by adjacent countries. Then again if desperate enough, why not launch an untested device.

The nightmare scenario was building in momentum, with many military chiefs advocating pre-emptive strikes, leading to readiness for a full nuclear war.

Many Zone leaders were desperate to confide in other Zone leaders. But with such paranoia it really was impossible to know if any request for co-operation might be seen as weakness, which could be exploited. The result, stalemate, no meaningful dialogue.

Each Zone leader was grandstanding, appearing defiant and resolute whilst appeasing condescendingly. Their Military Chiefs, with pseudo determination. What a dangerous, precarious and unsustainable farce.

Then at last a breakthrough, when the Homeland Defence chief of Zone 001, suggested an electronic Forum where ideas and suggestions would be posted for all Zone leaders to see. All Zones certainly had the technology with the ability to encrypt the IP sources of those sending ideas, and those reading and responding would also be completely secret.

The scheme was simply called Forum 2060.

This way, an idea would receive a voting status on relevance, appeal and acceptability.

Once an idea had been accepted in principle, then solutions would be posted and voted upon. This could work, yes it really could, with no one loosing face and the world's top brains all contributing.

It took only three days for the heavily encrypted internet to be established with an interactive screen set up in each Zone's Ministry of Information.

No other linkage was allowed to the dedicated lines, for to have any level of hacking would be disastrous, especially if the hackers were the very people perpetuating this panic by moving the illegal ^{235}U around the world. It was clear to all Zone leaders that a terrorist group had formed with bases in several Zones and somehow they had found a way to communicate to perpetrate this outrage.

But no organisation was coming forward to claim responsibility, and so the notion of extremists pursuing a cause, an ideology, was now questionable.

These must be fanatics, extreme in their thinking. As a nuclear war would leave no one alive on the planet to understand let alone embrace, change. Reformation in any guise would be pointless.

Trying to make any sense of the motivation of these perceived fanatics was only exacerbating all efforts.

This great opportunity immediately stalled when everyone was invited to state precisely what the problem was. It may seem glaringly obvious that it is "The coming and going of quantities of ^{235}U".

But how is that a problem, capable of being solved. Surely, many argued, the first question must be more precise. For example, how did ^{235}U formally identified form the al-Dabaa plant become enriched to ^{235}U and transported to eight Zones.

This was not such an erroneous question, as the process of enrichment is very precise and must be controlled throughout. Surely this must be the starting point, many argued.

Other Zones advocated containment, then realized that the illegal ^{235}U had disappeared again. And even if they could located all eight packages, then what guarantee could be given it would again not be taken surreptitiously. The great Forum 2060 idea had stalled.

The huge screens in each Ministry of Information flickered day and night, showing no messages, and so the scheme was given just a further 36 hours before switch off.

This abandoned idea had just made matters worse.

The countdown was hardly noticed as the hours passed and each Zone became more engrossed in defence and attack strategies.

What was really alarming was that the engineers at each ICBM silo and air force base were re- commissioning their long term mothballed bombers and fighters.

With so much aggression for war footing, it must surely only be a matter of hours before some irresponsible idiot gives the order to launch.

The retaliation would be immediate and indiscriminate setting the chain reaction underway. The world would be destroyed in a matter of hours, a day at most.

Even the cessation of bombing, at some mid stage would be pointless, for the physical damage and resulting radioactive fallout would destroy mankind. If not in days, then weeks and for remote locations, maybe a couple of months.

Truly a nuclear winter and eventual Armageddon.

The nuclear defence and fall out shelters each Zone had built would be futile, unless they could procreate families for at least a hundred years before surfacing.

No one was stopping to ask what the hell would be the point of destroying each other. For surely that has to be what terrorists want. So by initiating a nuclear all out war are the Zones not doing the job for them,

If so, these unknown terrorists have won. How completely and utterly bloody pointless, is that?

The pacifists, or doves, in each Zone were screaming out his message, all the time it falling on deaf ears. For the defensive arrogance of many Zone leaders blinded them to reason, common sense and compromise.

Then there were the hawks, who quite simply wanted war. Thinking the very threat would cause the other Zones to capitulate. This madness has to be seen to be believed.

Total world annihilation, rather than compromise.

Then the anticipated and dreaded event occurred.

Zone 140 fired a short range missile into Zone 98. It was intercepted by a ground to air missile and thankfully caused minimal collateral damage. Zone 98 wasted no time in using Forum 2060 to tell the world what had happened.

Zone 140 was threatened that another attack would result in deliberate pin point retaliation on them from at least ten Zones. The weapons would be conventional but substantial. This threat had reverberations around the world and was exactly what was needed for Zone leaders to settle down and regain reason.

Zone 140 suffered serious internal repercussions, as three of the Zone leaders committed suicide and four others were found killed in their homes. Maybe the outrageous action by Zone 140 was exactly what was needed at that time, to have a global impact.

The Format 2060 screens had less that ten hours to switch off, when a message appeared.

"Urgent message : dangerous consignment located in store TX-007-M." once again in the main warehouse at the al-Dabaa nuclear power plant.

The doomsday scenario has returned. It is back !

Chapter 6.
Action Day countdown.

Parveen, Aaheru, Monique and Dhul Fiqaar had been convening lay-person meetings to find, if not solutions, then at least answers to questions or ideas.

It really had been a waste of time, for the groups seemed incapable, at best reluctant, to understand what was being asked of them. Most found it incredulous that weapons grade uranium could be misplaced or lost. Only to appear again.

This shattered their fragile confidence in the security and safety of the plant. That on top of the endless dictatorial political controls and social restrictions, seemed too much to take. A total contradiction.

They were incapable of concentrating on the actual problem, seeing only a disaster waiting to unfold, with catastrophic outcomes. This made them all intellectually impotent.

Within a few days the layperson brainstorming groups were disbanded.

The news that the presumably the Presence had proclaimed through Forum 2060:-

"Urgent message : dangerous consignment located in store TX-007-M" galvanised the Facilitators back into action at the plant. Sure enough 2½ kilograms of ^{235}U was there in storage, in the same location as before.

It was a forgone conclusion that the other eight packages would have likewise returned, which was quickly substantiated. So the cat and mouse game was on again.

This apparent flippancy could be turned to advantage if it could be proven that something mischievous was behind this situation. Could the Facilitators convince their masters that some form of dangerous manipulation was being perpetrated.

This change of emphasis from perceived nuclear threat to brinkmanship had to be concluded, as no evidence existed that the weapons grade uranium had been engineered into a nuclear bomb. For if it was happening somewhere, then where was the evidence.

It had been agreed that the reports from Parveen, Aaheru, Monique and Dhul Fiqaar, could and should be transmitted to designated persons in each Zone.

For it would be ludicrous for any development to be the reserve of a few, whilst the many were left unknowing and uncertain. That could lead to further paranoia.

So two essential activities were happening. One, to convince the Zone leaders that to wait would not of necessity be irresponsible and two, to find some way of communicating with the Presence.

The levels of security on the returning ^{235}U at all locations had been increased to 24/7 visual surveillance with movement and vibration monitoring. This required teams of four security personnel in close contact with the material, changing every four hours.

The only way that material could move would be if it was dematerialised and materialised again through molecular fragmentation.

Not a science known to man, at that time.

Returning to the question of convincing the Zone leaders to wait, was to make a personal appearance at the reconvened Beijing Summit. So this was arranged.

Should all four go, or should two remain to continue the investigations. Toss of a coin and Parveen, and Aaheru remained at the plant, whilst Monique and Dhul Fiqaar flew to Beijing.

Organised chaos again as the 147 Delegates arrived and settled in.

The Chairman Host had prepared an agenda which was basically ignored within an hour of the Summit opening.

Such was the frustration of so many Zone leaders that control could only be maintained by the Summit sound engineers switching on and off the microphones of Delegates, under the command of the Chairman.

This action further exacerbated the emotions of many and anger permeated the vast hall. This was no atmosphere for reason to pervade.

For lunch, a cold buffet, with agreeable wines, brought some measure of tranquillity to the affair and returning to the great hall an hour later, found most Delegates in a slightly more relaxed frame of mind.

All microphones turned back on, the Chairman invited ideas from the Delegates.

These ranged from, gathering all of the illegal ^{235}U and placing into sealed tombs at the bottom of the Atlantic ocean, to a complete rundown of all military preparations.

In fairness, most suggestions were well received and debated but securing any level of majority or unanimous acceptance, proved impossible.

This seesawing continued through to 8pm when the Chairman ended the day.

Monique and Dhul Fiqaar had watched on in wonder and disbelief at the antics of the people who ruled the now divided world. Is it any wonder this planet was now 147 autonomous Zones.

This situation threatened the entire globe and yet almost every motion put forward or tabled, was one of self preservation for Zones.

It became evident that forming Zones had only really enforced the idea and practice of fierce, parochial isolationism. It was no wonder they could not agree on even the simplest of proposals, yet alone something as monstrous as this.

For this Summit to have any success it was essential to find a common goal, that will appeal to all Zones.

One would have thought that global survival would have been enough for harmony and unison, not so. So what would appeal?

Money, commercial but realistic. But would that be divisive if a Zone were to receive substantial payment for finding the solution. Also who would provide the funds, as each Zone was penurious due to Zonalisation, which ended all cross border and global trading.

Many thought to wait to see if the heightened security of the eight illegal packages would be sufficient to put an end to the perceived terrorist plot.

Others countered that to wait, to prevaricate, would only allow any other clandestine activity to go undetected until it was too late.

There was even talk of certain Zones working in collaboration, these mainly being Zones with shared borders who had found policing their borders an impossible task.

But this only threw up the question of air space above Zones, which had never been tackled. Particularly because all flights had to be sanctioned at the most senior level in each Zone and notified to every other Zone, precisely because of the air space violation and obvious security risk questions.

So, limited collaboration of specified topics seem a possible compromise regarding information sharing only. But is this really progress ? or just desperate time wasting.

Mid morning on the third day of the Summit, Monique and Dhul Fiqaar were invited to address the Delegates. They had thought long and hard about this moment and had re scripted several times, often as a result of what had transpired in the great hall each day.

It was clearly pointless, discourteous and provocative to give the Delegates any form of challenge, or to state the obvious or to advocate policy.

There were so many no-go areas to consider during this address to the delegates.

So maybe the subtlety of thought promotion, where a statement slowly percolates into the minds of the delegates and the truth becomes self evident over a day or two.   So what seeds to sow, and how.

They had decided to discuss options and the viability of each without specifically identifying those advocates by Zone. Toying with the 'what-if' scenario option should bring some positive response that would hopefully start gelling the collective thought processes.

Dhul Fiqaar nervously started with some humour of the arrogant blonde flight passenger:-

A plane is on its way to Zone 27 when a blonde in Economy Class gets up and moves to the First Class section and sits down. The flight attendant watches her do this and asks to see her ticket. She then tells the blonde that she paid for Economy and that she will have to sit in the back. The blonde replies "I'm blonde, I'm beautiful, I'm going to Zone 27 and I'm staying here!"

The flight attendant goes into the cockpit and tells the pilot and co-pilot that there is some blonde bimbo sitting in First Class that belongs in Economy and won't move back to her seat. The co-pilot goes back to the Blonde and tries to explain that because she only paid for Economy she will have to leave and return to her seat.

The blonde replies, "I'm blonde, I'm beautiful, I'm going to Zone 27 and I'm staying right here!" The co-pilot tells the pilot that he probably should have the police waiting when they land to arrest this blonde woman that won't listen to reason. The pilot says, "You say she's blonde?, I'll handle this, I'm married to a blonde, I speak blonde!"

He goes back to the blonde, whispers in her ear, and she says "Oh, I'm sorry," gets up and moves back to her seat in the economy section. The flight attendant and co-pilot are amazed and asked him what he said to her.

"I told her First Class isn't going to Zone 27."

Though many years had passed since political correctness had ended, these type of derogatory comments about blonde ladies being of lesser intellect, pre-occupied with appearance and material gain; nevertheless the humour was well received.

A lessoning of tensions was palpable and Dhul Fiqaar wasted no time in his delivery.

His opening approach was a back to basics review of what had caused the world to form Zones.

The progressive disintegration of the world had many areas to consider, all very significant in their own right but when considered as a collective whole, the inevitable collapse or implosion was precisely that. The world could not sustain itself.

Most of mankind's revelations and mistakes leading to the formation of the Zones were based upon invention, not discovery. Man's curiosity and creative ability have led him to constantly challenge.

- Innovation not stagnation.

- New frontiers not established pastures.

- Leave nothing to rest, now a total pre-occupation.

From the elimination of birth defects and disease, to increased crop yields, housing and social engineering, right through to oceanography, sub terrain and space exploration, the so-called final frontier. There was nowhere that man would not go, with no subject left unchallenged.

Many traditional values and methods of working and materials were abandoned, as the world rushed headlong into a nebulous limbo of insatiable greed and blind fury.

Even the pace of living between town dwellers and those in rural retreats was no longer sacrosanct. Civilisations became obsolete along with their traditions, beliefs, ethics and historical identity.

This pulled religion into the vortex, being sucked down into the heart of the commercial and politically-correct, uncaring whirlpool.

There was so much pre-occupation with migration of different nationalities into every country that national identity became a by-word, obsolete and redundant.

As the world struggled to become international with multi cultural integration, so local resentments increased, dramatically and often violently.

People became heartedly sickened by being told that non indigenous peoples could take limited housing, jobs, schools, transport and financial support. Added to that they wanted to bring in their relatives.

And then once settled, they started to breed, often totally out of control. Sucking the economic and social service resource life's blood, out of their adopted countries.

Historians continue to try to apportion blame, responsibility, culpability for why the world descended into Zones. It is always someone else's fault, they should have seen it coming and changed course, or introduced legislation. Never did, for the world was so engrossed in being seen as the good guys, paranoid about bad press and hyper cautious about being critically reported, on the 24/7 news channels.

The press and broadcasting media were literally dictating government policy with every Ministry having a press secretary and media liaison officer. It was farcical and glaringly subservient to media dictates.

This was seriously compounded by the revelation that politicians of all persuasions were found to be defrauding the government through their personal expenses for both domestic and international duties.

News, every minute of every day and nearly always bad, depressing, negative, underlying the blame culture. Needing to point the finger and often glamorising appalling behaviour from criminals and many so-called celebrities, who advocate drug and alcohol related degenerate behaviour.

Sports people, one time heroes of societies now exposed as liars, drug takers, committing adultery, thieving, and cheating, even fixing sporting events.

The news medias always knew of worthwhile events in society but rarely chose to publish the goodness in the world. Choosing nearly always to report death, floods, malnutrition, droughts, earthquakes, tsunamis, wars, paedophilia, insurrections; anything that was cruel, crude and violent.

And the closer they could get their reporters and cameras crews to the actual event, the happier they were, celebrating with annual awards for their sick and overly glorified profession.

Monique, like many of her generation, grew up knowing traditional values from her infant, rural life, in France, to modern beliefs on the dispassionate streets of London, coupled with her global travels, as a Facilitator.

Like so many of her contemporaries, she made the only sustainable decision, that of selective memory.

There had been many interesting debates at the Facilitators training Ministry.

Indeed they were required to attend workshops that looked critically at developments in all Zones. Not just with regard to hostilities and threats, but also of cultural changes, the creation or rebirth of religions and changes that continued to shape the 147 Zones. They needed this awareness, for use on their travels.

The Facilitators were also required to produce hypotheses on the major factors impacting on, and changing the Zones. Commonality first then local idiosyncrasies and transitional needs.

These regular assessments became one of the rare activities that were shared between all Zones, on the basis of collective learning and risk containment.

Each Facilitator was asked to identify and comment upon major events or activities occurring around the fragmented world.

Then to assess each finding for benefits and problems. Time and again the reasons apportioned for global disharmony that lead to the creation of the Zones, were fairly evenly shared between:-

1. Information Technology : So much to answer for.

2. Cyber-terrorism

3. Confidentiality breakdown between world leaders.

4. Global warming

5. Economic meltdown legacy from 2008/9

6. The Continuing multiplicity of wars.

1. **Information Technology :**

So much to answer for. Two distinct schools of thought. Information Technology has contributed to the world. Or is taking away the privacy of normal people and breaking overall reputation of World Wide Human knowledge.

I.T. Pros:-
The world has increased flexibility with IT assisted communication systems.
The sense of responsibility has increased through networking sites.
Easy thinking and evolution in transportation through Search Engines.
Saves thousand of lives daily with diagnostic equipment and disease eradication.
Increase the sense of Human Rights with global events and developments.

I.T. Cons:-
It has taken away people's Privacy information access and opened abuse.
The online community is not safe for family anymore. Social abuses.
It is going to damage a Human's Natural Power.
Erosion of principles and ethics.
It can bring World Destruction without Efficient Administration.

Cyber-terrorism.
Is a phrase used to describe the use of Internet based attacks in terrorist activities, including acts of deliberate, large-scale disruption of computer networks, especially of personal computers attached to the Internet, by the means of tools such as computer viruses.

Cyber-terrorism can also be defined much more generally as any computer crime targeting computer networks without necessarily affecting real world infrastructure, property, or lives.

Narrow definition.   If treated similarly to traditional terrorism, then it only includes attacks that threaten property or lives, and can be defined as the leveraging of a target's computers and information, particularly via the Internet, to cause physical, real-world harm or severe disruption of infrastructure.

For 'Doomsday' scenario awareness and preventative planning, the Facilitators are regularly questioned on the ten most likely events that could endanger mankind.

The results are predictable and rarely change in ranking.

In reverse order the Facilitators agreed:-

10) Oil Crash.   Prediction of a peak oil crisis, where fossil fuels dry up, triggering an economic meltdown followed by the collapse of the agricultural system and mass starvation.

9) Cyberterrorism.   Historically terrorists needed explosives. Now all that is needed is an iPad. With the click of a mouse, whether religious zealots, political activists, or mischievous teenage hackers - can deploy nefarious computer worms that bring down power plants, hospital equipment, even nuclear facilities.

8) A New Disease.   Not only are many deadly diseases developing immunity to drugs, but global warming could thaw out some virulent disease from the past, such as the 1918-1919 flu - which killed 50 million - and new viruses could even filter down from outer space.

7) Day of Judgements or Reckoning has passed so many times. The last forecast major event was back in 2012 which is the last day on the Mayan long-count calendar when the sun will erupt in a super-storm and destroy all life on Earth.

6) Nuclear Catastrophe.   As unstable states expand their nuclear programs, the risk of nuclear war is as great as ever and is increasing exponentially. Whether humans could survive a nuclear winter - the severe cold and diminished sunlight that would follow such a war.

5) Global Warming.   For decades there has been the debate on how much humans are to blame for global warming, but in the last forty

years, climate-related disasters such as flooding and droughts have affected over three billion people. It's thought that global warming could eventually turn Earth into a planet like Venus, where, greenhouse-effect temperatures are sufficient to melt lead.

4) Overpopulation.   The world population is growing by about seventy four million a year. The UN predicted and it has been realised that it will reach nine billion people by 2060. Overpopulation could eventually lead to crop failure and starvation.

3) Cosmic Doom.   Working from the belief that dinosaurs became extinct after a massive asteroid hit the earth 65 million years ago. The possibility of this recurring again is a mathematical fact. Other threats include black holes and the heat death of the universe.

2) Superhuman Uprising.   If humans get overzealous with genetic modification, could we accidentally engineer an organism that rapidly reproduces and takes over the earth? In 2060 this is now a controlled reality.

1) Robots Replacing People.   Nanotechnology has been developed significantly with a serious threat of out-of-control self-replicating robots that could consume all living matter on Earth.

2.   Confidentiality loss between world leaders.

WikiLeaks is a non-profit media organization dedicated to bringing important news and information to the public. They provide an innovative, secure and anonymous way for independent sources around the world to leak information to journalists. They publish material of ethical, political and historical significance while keeping the identity of sources anonymous, thus providing a universal way for the revealing of suppressed and censored injustices.

It publishes submissions of otherwise unavailable documents from anonymous news sources and news leaks. Within a year of its launch, the site claimed a database that had grown to more than 1.2 million documents. Now it has billions of classified documents.

Though global in its indiscriminate outgoings, it does concentrate on the USA and continues to publish sensitive documents and film footage, once thought to be highly classified if not 'Secret'.

This has brought paranoia across many countries and at all levels. From Kings to Presidents right through the hierarchy of ambassadors, diplomats and civil servants. Despite fierce opposition, it continues today. The site remains available on multiple servers and different domain names following a number of denial-of-service attacks and its severance from different Domain Name System (DNS) providers.

3. Global warming.

For many years the Intergovernmental Panel on Climate Change (IPCC) state that leading climate scientists are certain that human activity is heating up the planet. A hypothesis that had been contested since the 1980's.

Greenhouse gases increased due to the consumption of fossil fuels, new forms of land use, and agriculture. Whilst atmospheric pollution has had a cooling effect.

The main climate changes have been observed in Arctic temperatures and ice, widespread changes in precipitation amounts, ocean salinity, wind patterns and aspects of extreme weather including droughts, heavy precipitation, heat waves and the intensity of tropical cyclones.

Critics refer to changes in the sun's radiation to account for global warming. Although there are fluctuations in the sun's radiation, its effects are nearly 20 times weaker than human-induced warming.

4. Economic meltdown legacy from 2008/9

The financial crisis was triggered by a liquidity shortfall in the United States banking system. It resulted in the collapse of large financial institutions, the bailout of banks by national governments, and downturns in stock markets around the world. In many areas, the housing market also suffered, resulting in evictions, foreclosures and prolonged vacancies.

The collapse of the housing bubble, which peaked in the U.S. in 2006, caused the values of securities tied to real estate pricing to plummet thereafter, damaging financial institutions globally.

Questions regarding bank solvency, declines in credit availability, and damaged investor confidence had an impact on global stock markets, where securities suffered large losses during late 2008 and early 2009.

One of the long-term worldwide consequences of the economic breakdown was the European sovereign debt crisis. That crisis primarily impacted Greece, Ireland, Portugal, Italy, and Spain. The governments of these nations habitually run large government budget deficits.

Other Eurozone countries also suffered from bad governing with widespread corruption and tax evasion.

A doomsday event

is a specific, plausibly verifiable or hypothetical occurrence which has an exceptionally destructive effect on the human race. The final outcomes of doomsday events may range from a major disruption of human civilization, the extinction of humanity, the extinction of all life on the planet Earth, the destruction of the planet Earth, the annihilation of the Solar system, to the annihilation of our galaxy or even the entire universe.

Even though the term "doomsday" is taken from Christian eschatology referring to the Last Judgment, the term "doomsday event" as used here refers to alleged realistic dangers from natural or man-made causes, to be distinguished from catastrophic events in religious eschatology understood as an act of divine retribution or unalterable fate.

Dhul Fiqaar continued with the summit leaders:-

- What if we do nothing. ?

- Why should we do something. ?

- Is it because it is expected of us as Zone leaders and Facilitators. ?

This subtle alignment was not wasted on Monique, as Dhul Fiqaar continued with the relationship building.

He wanted to be seen as one of them, to gain attention and credibility, and it was working.

The Delegates soon responded with ideas and suggestions rather than questions and criticisms. Even with the crescent seating configuration in the great hall, Delegates started turning to converse with other.

Monique's approach was to leave the Delegates with less fear and apprehension. This she achieved by stating that despite the global fears, no one, except the regrettable situation in Zone 140, had been injured or worse, killed.

Reminding everyone that the fundamental problem was the potential for violent outbreaks of war. But if war seemed such an inevitable con-sequence, then why not restrict such a conflict to conventional weapons.

She argued that at present eight illegal packages existed and that each was under 24/7 surveillance, and that none had, or would be, built into a nuclear bomb.

What if all Zones declared a moratorium on nuclear weapon use, using the Facilitators to ensure continued compliance.

After all, isn't that the primary duty of the Facilitators.

Great idea, but was it do-able. Would all Zones sign up to such an agreement and more importantly, honour it, without any open or veiled threat of enforcement.

Monique and Dhul Fiqaar thanked the Delegates for their kind attention and understanding then left Beijing to return to al-Dabaa, to find out what progress Parveen and Aaheru had made.

It came as disappointing but no surprise, that advances had not been possible. The safeguarded package was still there and intact. No other findings of illegal packages had been reported in any other Zone.

Could Parveen, Aaheru, Monique and Dhul Fiqaar now pack up, and go back to their Zones. As tempting as this thought was, unless so ordered by their masters or given another assignment they all agreed to stay, though they had not a single idea of what to do next.

Chapter 7.
The Presence.

The days that followed were empty and yet somehow relaxing. For so long, they had been under the hammer for answers from totally unreasonable masters, colleagues and plant staff.

That's the problem with putting ourselves up as special people, with superior capabilities.

It is okay to revel in the spotlight when problems are straight forward and solutions easily found. The truth is that up to this horrendous problem, none of them had ever really been tested.

Maybe that realisation added to their discomfort at being little more than average. An observation that had not been missed by their Zone leaders.

In Zone 004 with a dwindling population of 34 million down from 62 million in the early 21st century, the number of Facilitators was 64. This is one Facilitator per half a million population.

No wonder a certain arrogance existed amongst Facilitators. For so long they had been special.

But now, reduced to having to accept that they had failed miserably, was indeed sobering and at the same time, outright challenging.

Damned if this is going to beat us they vowed and took a radical decision. They were going to try to contact the Presence, if it even existed, and if it was in any way involved in the illegal packages of uranium.

But where to start. How the hell do you contact something that may not there. This Presence had never been seen, heard or felt, in the physical sense.

And yet Parveen, Aaheru, Monique and Dhul Fiqaar would not deny their experiences when the Presence visited. Was it a coincidence that the Presence happened shortly after the illegal packages started and if so, then what the heck does it want, if anything.

Nevertheless it was a starting point in what had been a fruitless exercise so far. A feeling of nothing to lose, lots to gain, including credibility. Ego and pride again, so watch it people !

The Presence; so where to begin. They could hardly issue an invitation and yet was it their vulnerability, the opening it wanted, they puzzled. When they were at their lowest it appeared, albeit as some form of energy field or maybe as a mental apparition. The fact that it defies description, does not mean it does not exist.

Or is it deeply embedded in our sub-conscious and do other people have these experiences, but are reluctant to speak about them publicly.

Many years ago flat-liner experiments with near death threshold exposures resulted in people returning to consciousness and talking of such things. The endorphins released by the body under certain threatening conditions can have a profound hallucinogenic effect.

So what is the difference between fact and fiction.

Experiences ranging from out of body, to walking to heaven. Feelings of immortality and invincibility. Extreme emotions ranging from ecstasy to terror. Without any external stimulus thus demonstrating that our mind is capable of amazing things.

Before attempting to contact the Presence, Parveen, Dhul Fiqaar, Aaheru and Monique all agreed some serious research was needed. But where to begin for they certainly had direct access to the most powerful databases on the planet.

So they typed in "The Human Brain.- Mind Control.- Periods of Experimentation."

Back to absolutely first principles, they agreed, no presumption or assumption. Starting point is:-

The brain is the centre of the nervous system.

The cerebral cortex of the human brain contains 15–33 billion neurons, linked with up to 10,000 synaptic connections each.

These neurons communicate with one another by means of long protoplasmic fibres called axons.

That's the physiology considered, now what about capabilities and susceptibility to external influences.

There first readings considered the work of:-

Robert Monroe, founder of The Monroe Institute in Faber, Virginia, USA. He is best known for Monroe's Big Discovery.

His early research was initially designed to determine the feasibility of learning during sleep, but in 1958, an astonishing result emerged. By experimenting with the effects of sonic frequencies on the brain, Monroe successfully isolated a little-known state of awareness which was totally separated from the physical body. Called an Out-of-Body Experience.

The sonic principle was known to electronic engineers as binaural beat frequency modulation. However, Monroe applied this to bioelectronics, calling it Hemispherical Synchronization.

To achieve these mind-states, Monroe recorded two channels of audio data using a stereo tape recorder. On one channel he recorded a frequency of 200 cycles per second (cps), and on the other channel he recorded a frequency of 208 cps. When he played the recordings back through a pair of stereo headphones, what Monroe discovered was that while one ear heard the 200 cps tone, and the other ear heard the 208 tone, the brain interpreted the tones as an eight cps frequency, and began to entrain itself to that frequency. In other words, the brain could only distinguish the eight cps difference, and this frequency was powerful enough to entrain brainwaves.

1998, Vic Tandy, Psychical Research. It has been cited that infrasound [sound below 20 Hz, which cannot be heard by humans but can be felt as vibration].

This was the cause of apparitions seen by him seeing a so-called haunting in a laboratory in Warwick.

When he measured the infrasound in the laboratory, the showing was 18.98 hertz--the exact frequency at which a human eyeball starts resonating. The sound waves made his eyeballs resonate and produced optical illusions, making him see a figure that didn't exist.

Infrasonic waves can carry over long distances and are less susceptible to disturbance or interference than higher frequencies

Resonance frequencies. One of the great revelations of 20th century science is that all existence can be broken down into simple wave functions. Every photon, energy emission, and elementary particle rings with its own unique wave signature. Even the neurochemical processes of human consciousness, our very thoughts, ring with their own distinct wave patterns.

By studying the way that waves interact with other waves, researchers had found that even low-powered oscillations can have enormous effects on standing waves, physical structures, and even the human brain.

The principle which describes this particular wavelength interaction is known as resonance. When you resonate with something, you are emitting a wave signature which is "in sync" with it. By applying a constant resonant frequency to a standing wave, you can intensify, reinforce, and prolong the standing frequency of that wave. Researchers posit that by applying these concepts of resonance to waves emitted by the brain, it is possible to induce altered brain states.

James Casbolt (2008) had written on secret government operations and NSA mind control operation called Project Mannequin.

He contended there were over 400 Deep Underground Military Bases worldwide. He also claims thousands of adults and children are brutalised, tortured, programmed, experimented upon, and killed in those underground facilities, with some taken by aliens.

Manipulation of the masses by cloning, total mind control, invisibility, anti-gravity, free energy, age regression, soul transfers, extended life spans, time travel, space portals, ability to cure any disease, time machines, etc. are already in the hands of the military.

That, he claimed, leads to a New World Order run by alien overlords with subordinate and subservient humans. The NWO/alien agenda includes eliminating about 85% of the world's population (wars, chemtrails, vaccines, engineered diseases, engineered hurricanes and earthquakes, etc) so there won't be enough humans left on the planet to offer any meaningful resistance when the Dracos invasion is in full swing.

Were these the ramblings of a deranged individual or an inevitable prophecy.

Dr. Joseph Mengele of Auschwitz notoriety was the principle developer of the trauma-based Monarch Project and the CIA's MK Ultra mind control programs. Mengele and approximately 5, 000 other high ranking Nazis were secretly moved into the United States and South America in the aftermath of World War II, in an Operation designated 'Paperclip'.

The Nazis continued their work in developing mind control and rocketry technologies in secret underground military bases. The only thing made public was the rocketry work with former Nazi so-called celebrities like Warner Von Braun.

The killers, torturers, and mutilators of innocent human beings were kept discretely out of sight, but busy in U.S. underground military facilities which gradually became home to many thousands of kidnapped American children snatched off the streets (about one million per year) and placed into iron bar cages stacked from floor to ceiling as part of the 'training'.

These children would be used to further refine and perfect Mengele's mind control technologies.

Certain selected children, at least the ones who survived the 'training' would become future mind controlled slaves who could be used for different jobs ranging anywhere from sexual slavery to assassinations.

A substantial portion of these children, who were considered expendable, were intentionally slaughtered in front of, and by, the other children, in order to traumatize trainees into compliance and submission.

Criticism and self-criticism in the Korean War involved sessions held for the American prisoners of war by the Chinese that clearly had deeper effects than the POWs could initially comprehend. Initially prisoners found this childish, but without them being able to realize it, the situation of being subjected constantly to the criticism of one's comrades became humiliating.

That adults should publicly discuss habits or inclinations, some of a very private nature, confess one's faults, receive strong criticism for insignificant misdemeanours. This continuing humiliation became crucial in the gradual psychological break-up of the prisoners' personalities. Furthermore, this ongoing process was bound to cause mistrust for their comrades: called "divide and conquer" by the ancient Romans. And applied during China's "Cultural Revolution" as a method of "re-education".

The topic of mind control is elaborate, multifaceted, and multi layered. But why have any form of mind control. One application was the plan to create a mind controlled workers society. Advanced horrendously in the WW2 Nazi concentration camps when an unlimited supply of children and adults were available for experimentation.

Trauma-based or electronic-based. Mind control technologies can be broadly divided into two subsets:

The first phase of government mind control development grew out of the old occult techniques which required the victim to be exposed to massive psychological and physical trauma.

This usually began in infancy, in order to cause the psyche to shatter into a thousand alter personalities which can then be separately programmed to perform any function that the programmer wishes to "install".

Each alter personality created is separate and distinct from the front personality. The 'front personality' is unaware of the existence or activities of the alter personalities. Alter personalities can be brought to the surface by programmers or handlers using special codes. The victim of mind control can also be affected by specific sounds, words, or actions known as triggers.

The second phase of mind control development was refined at an underground base below Fort Hero on Montauk , Long Island (New York) and is referred to as the Montauk Project.

The earliest adolescent victims of Montauk style programming, so called Montauk Boys, were programmed using trauma-based techniques, but that method was eventually abandoned in favour of an all-electronic induction process which could be "installed" in a matter of days, or even hours, instead of the many years that it took to complete trauma-based methods.

The Facilitators invested many hours of reading with line by line analytical research. They have been trained to be methodical and relentless. But once again, the real potential for information overload existed with the possibility of missing simple but important facts.

From all of this research not one hypothesis could be applied into the burning question of the Presence reality.

Of the four, Parveen, Dhul Fiqaar, Aaheru and Monique, Aaheru was the most proficient.

His razor sharp analytical mind was pragmatism personified. With this came a serious attitude problem , born out of intolerance, and many times he would challenge his colleagues, confront them, criticise and complain about their lethargy.

Jesus what a fucking pain in the arse, but equally what an invaluable asset, especially on an exercise like this.

Parveen, Dhul Fiqaar and Monique all conceded.

It was Aaheru who pointed out that all four were reacting to sensations about the Presence. So, which of their senses were reacting and was it in any particular order or level of sensitivity.

He wanted to confirm or eliminate if their senses were being manipulated, orchestrated, configured, or shaped into a predetermined response.

Initially the other three were totally confused and gave little more than ridicule.

So, he repeated, which senses, the order and strength. Everyone accepted it was not touch, sight, hearing or smell this just leaves taste, which was equally and obviously rejected. Christ, they hadn't eaten the thing.

So how did they know for certain the Presence was in fact present and that it was not a form of mind control.

Aaheru was by now convinced that the answer lay in the work of Vic Tandy, Psychical Research and the profound effect of Resonant Frequencies, on the human mind and body.

He proposed that the Presence was at this time simply trying to connect, communicate, affect an awareness, call it what you like. Clearly it was working, if only in part as witnessed by the fact that the Facilitators all agreed on the existence of the Presence.

So at last a break through, no matter how tenuous. Though still unclear, it did give the Facilitators a strange feeling of déjà-vu; a genesis to the final solution and hopefully the salvation of this paranoid, troubled world.

A good night's sleep followed, at last. They agreed to keep their investigations away from their Zone masters who at least for now seemed pre-occupied with their own survival plans.

Even this little respite came as great relief.

All agreed that during the night would be the right time to establish contact.

Question, should it be just one of them, or all together, giving a collective mental receptor.

Four times the ability to sense and respond. That must be the way forward.

They were now hardly appearing back at the plant, much to the consternation of the plant management who were very unhappy at the whole situation.

Made worse by having four Facilitators on the problem with no results, or even theories to work with. Several Directors were still smarting at the incarceration of the Production Director, for standing up to Monique.

The Facilitators decided on the Transcendental Meditation (TM) technique. Nothing more stressful as it only involves a natural, effortless procedure while relaxing comfortably with the eyes closed.

Not being a religion, philosophy, or lifestyle, it is as an effective method of self-development.

Transcendental Meditation allows the Facilitators to settle inward beyond thought, to experience the source of thought, pure awareness, transcendental consciousness, or, the unified field.

This brings on a silent and peaceful level of consciousness, the innermost Self. In this state of restful alertness, the brain functions with significantly greater coherence and the body gains deep rest.

Transcendental Meditation is based on the ancient Vedic tradition of enlightenment in India. This knowledge has been handed down by Vedic masters for thousands of years. Restoring the knowledge and experience of higher states of consciousness so using the same procedures for maximum effectiveness.

TM allows the mind to simply, naturally and effortlessly transcend thinking and to experience a deep state of restfully alert consciousness, giving holistic benefits.

They are also hoping it will liberate their minds to be fully receptive to any attempt at contact by the Presence.

A night time exercise then. Wrapping up warm they drove out from the hotel by about five kilometres and parked up near a disused roadside 'sheesha' house.

The bodyguards insisted this behaviour, which required them to keep well away, was given as written authority. They argued it was irresponsible and reckless.

Being a bodyguard to a Facilitator was seen as a very prestigious appointment. Exceptional in mind and body.

Many held that bodyguards had been brainwashed to remove any thoughts of survival or to consider fear of harm. They were nevertheless sworn to secrecy and loyalty to the Facilitators, at any cost.

Since the formation of the Facilitators it is estimated that over one hundred bodyguards had perished, mainly in the early years as politicians, terrorists, extremists or just normal people challenged or resisted the introduction of the Facilitators. There was no data on how many civilians had been detained or even worse by the bodyguards. Zone secrets prevented this.

This made the Facilitators a force to be obeyed and avoided, if there was a clash of ideology or a resistance to accepting their rulings. The protester would suffer.

Out of their warm car, they chose a spot at the rear of the dilapidated building. A blanket was laid on the ground, cushions scattered and a wee dram of a most agreeable cognac eagerly passed around. They were extremely apprehensive but actually, feeling pretty good at the prospect of progress.

What next, do they hold hands, sit in a square or as much of a circle as they can form. Does someone ask out loud if there is a presence. Do they close their eyes or stare into the cold night sky.

Do they all do the same thing in unison or should each seek their own comfort level, posture and breathing rhythm. Surely they needed collective consciousness.

It was turning into a farce after all. A nervous cough, followed by another. Someone smirked, then chuckled which was fatal, as it became contagious with all four laughing uncontrollably within a few minutes.

So much for the disciplines and opportunities from Transcendental Meditation which was clearly inappropriate for this situation.

What did they look like. Four of the planets most highly trained and disciplined people acting like they're on a youth club, weekend excursion.

Thank Christ no one could see them.

More cognac, and resigned sighs as they gathered up the ground covering and walked toward the car. Their eyes darting, from one to another, looking for an expression of retained dignity and determination, salvaged from the farce, as it will be remembered, for sure.

Four doors clunked shut. The security card pressed into the start slot, the near silent engine purred into life and a comforting voice asked for instructions.

The name of the hotel was all that was required and the car released the braking system and started to roll forward. This evening finished soon then they agreed.

The people transporter had not travel but a few metres when it suddenly stopped. Monique pressed the security card again, to no avail. The instruments confirmed the engine had stopped and would not restart, despite several attempts.

They reached for the access opening pads on each door. Nothing, the doors would not open but the car's power pack status showed full. No running engine meant no heat and they were not able to egress the car. This was worrying, becoming alarming. Fuck ! why did we dismiss the bodyguards they thought.

Think, just think. Of course, their communicators. Near panic, despite their disciplined training.

Parveen and Dhul Fiqaar both dialled up code 3. This meant that attention and contact was required via the supposedly defunct GPS system. All Facilitators had a 24/7 up and down highly encrypted link.

This was always instantaneous with the display requiring a coded input and a thumb print onto the identification pad. Crude but effective.

Finally a voice test by repeating a constantly changing message, given on the display.

Seconds passed, nothing. They tried again. Again, nothing. They tried a Code 2 input which meant they were in danger. Again nothing, despite three attempts.

A code 1 had never been tried, for it meant an episode so serious that the Security Ministries of all Zones would be linked in. Christ ! surely we do not have to send that.

An uncomfortable silence fell over the four as confusion mixed with apprehension scrambled their thoughts. Surely to goodness with their collective training and experience, then a solution must be forthcoming.

No one spoke as the temperature rapidly dropped and their breath formed dancing clouds to condensation droplets, on the icy windows.

Parveen kept trying her car door, but without handles, levers, buttons or switches then all efforts were in vain. This led to anger as she kicked at the door and thumped her clenched fists on the glass. She looked at the men in sad despair, thinking their physical superiority should have a direct bearing on their predicament. Alas no, as they too sat in adolescent contemplation.

Then it happened. A gentle rocking of the car initially, barely discernable but then increasing in intensity until a positive surge was felt. This caused all to look helplessly at each other, for an explanation.

They reached for each other and clasped hands, hugging where close enough, for they were certain this event must end in tragedy. Primeval fear permeated the car.

The car moved from side to side in a gentle oscillation and felt as if it had left the ground and then started to slowly rotate. Rational thoughts of a seismic earth tremor were quickly abandoned as the motions increased in intensity and frequency.

They were now little more than ping pong balls being bounced and thrown by the energy controlling the car. All thoughts of the cold now forgotten, they shouted and screamed in desperate panic praying this would end.

Their panic precluded any rational realisation that the car was gently pulsating. The oscillations and rotation of the car slowed and slowed until all movement stopped, and the car came to a rest.

Looks of utter disbelief on their faces. Logic was irrelevant and distracting. The glow came into their senses and a realisation that the extreme cold was no longer. They were neither cold or hot, fearful or calm, tense or relaxed. They were devoid of all feelings.

Incoherent mumblings is all they could muster as no one ventured a meaningful comment.

Suddenly the four doors unlocked and slowly opened, inviting freedom from the car. And yet no one hurried outside, they just sat there trans-fixed, nonplus and indifferent. Most significantly, they were all afraid.

The ever rational Dhul Fiqaar made the first move, taking three tentative steps away from the car, looking all around still in disbelief and summoning his colleagues to join him. The four of them just stood like helpless children.

It took several minutes for them to realise they were not alone, well maybe in the metaphysical sense they were but of course nothing could be seen or heard.

And yet each knew the Presence had most certainly made contact but in an infuriating one-way manner that caused panic, anger and confusion.

Hardly the start to a perfect relationship, silently mouthed Monique.

Aaheru having gathered his senses quicker than the rest suggested, as they were now standing outside the car, that maybe the machine was once again working. Within a few seconds all were seated and the security start card had the engine operating with a dazzling display of illuminated instruments, and a reassuring warm airflow.

The ride back to the hotel was in total silence. No one daring to put forward any attempt at an explanation. The eight bodyguards came running up to them in alarm.

"Where they heck have you been?" they demanded. It is three days since we last saw you and so we have contacted our Ministries of Security. They have given us just another twelve hours before a full security clamp down affecting all Facilitators would be actioned.

Parveen, Dhul Fiqaar, Aaheru and Monique had no answers and found themselves apologising for their seemingly cavalier attitude, promising it would never happen again.

But now more bloody problems. What did the bodyguards mean they had been missing for three days. That's complete bloody rubbish they agreed. No more than six hours, tops.

And the fucking Ministries have been notified. After everything else, that's all we need, for there will be courts of enquiry.

In the early days of the Facilitators there had been odd scares, and the response and fallout a nightmare that led to resignations and incarceration of politicians and Facilitators. What would be their fate, and how long before being summoned back to their Zones, to give a full account.

First priority now was to get the Ministries of Security off their backs. So what story line can we spin, contrived, but with the possibility of plausibility.

Monique suggested they had taken off to have peace and quiet to pursue alternatives and that they had taken food, drink and a change of clothing. But to leave every bodyguard behind would not be acceptable and they knew they would face sanctions for that.

But it was hoped, that at least it would keep the four together, to continue trying to resolve this enigma.

96

It worked and with the promise of severe sanctions against each of them on return, their Ministries authorised continued working.

They knew having made contact with the Presence that this had to be pursued rigorously now and so they hatched their latest plan, for they had convinced themselves that the illegal ^{235}U material appearances and the Presence were intrinsically linked.

Chapter 8.
Proof of a plot.

Parveen, Monique, Dhul Fiqaar and Aaheru had up to now accepted each as equals but clearly, as in all groups, this is simply not true. Especially for a given set of circumstances.

This is where the split in the group of four Facilitators started. For two wanted to pursue the logic path and the other two, a speculative, free-fall approach.

They argued at length, wasting valuable hours but a necessary time, in this investigation. For without a harmonious and co-ordinated approach, they would stagnate or even worse, regress. So they needed all four minds working.

They could not take the dilemma outside of the group for arbitration. This had not to be shared with another living soul.

Thing is you see, they didn't know if the Presence was only contacting them. Was there only one Presence or several. If several, then was what was happening to them also happening to other groups around the world, involving other Facilitators or normal citizens.

Again more bloody questions than answers.

But if they remain totally clandestine then they would probably never find out and would that constitute a lost opportunity for more minds to contribute.

And how long before one or more of the bodyguards found out what is happening. The bodyguards had been ordered to keep the Facilitators in sight at all times, sparing sleep and ablution essentials.

Parveen suggested they send out a coded message to other Facilitators. The encoded message read:-

"Subject:- illegal materials ^{235}U update.

Unexplained force field reported by technicians in the Zone 108 nuclear plant located at al-Dabaa." "Have there been any similar reports in your Zones ?"

This seemed innocuous enough they thought, and should bring some level of response if only to report no. Or even if this led to requests for further information.

However, they didn't want to start a dialogue for that would blow the lid of their scheming. But with so many other Facilitators out there, it would be ludicrous not to reach out.

The world still operated formalised time Zones.

So twelve hours either side of their transmission time would be needed and a thirty six hours wait, was agreed. A logical compromise to enable response.

The responses certainly came but mainly in the form of the need for more information. What did they mean by a force field. Was it electrical, magnetic, thermal, low level radioactive, sound, light, within the normal spectrum or varying wavelengths. Was the force field measureable and had any phenomenon been recorded.

Did the force field manifestation occur at the same time, same place and had it been reported by the same people. If so who were these people and did they have an agenda. Endless questions.

Hundreds of replies with the same repeated questions with one exception. Facilitator Lenechka from Zone 014 (Formally Russia). His reply was interesting in that he did not want to identify the type of force field only if the force field had in fact been experienced by any of the Facilitators there in Zone 108.

He avoided any reference to the technicians, effectively dismissing them from the question.

How to answer this oblique question. "Been experienced", he had asked. They decided to reply by saying that their level of belief in what they had been told, was tangible.

Within 24 hours Lenechka had joined then. Now there were five Facilitators. An unprecedented number of these specialists in one place, on one mission.

The same problem arose with regard to Lenechka's manner and attitude, very precise and uncompromising, to a point that was, by most standards, bloody rude.

Dhul Fiqaar and Aaheru were uneasy with Lenechka for a few days. Macho bullshit, commented Parveen. For goodness sake we are all Facilitators and we have the Mother and Father of a problem here, so what's the point of having resentment.

It is true Lenechka's attitude was humourless and precise. Sometimes smarmy, rarely giving eye contact, no hand shaking or any measure of tactility. Difficult to like someone like that, maybe he should just fuck off back to Zone 014.

Not the attitude insisted Monique and reasoned with Lenechka to ease up and become more approachable.

Seems Lenechka likes Vodka, now there's a surprise. Some things never change and a few of these heart warmers inside him, had a most marked relaxing affect.

Parveen, Monique, Dhul Fiqaar, Aaheru enjoyed the cognac and in the privacy of Aaheru's bedroom they shared with Lenechka their individual and shared experiences of the Presence and the ^{235}U packages.

Their revelations brought a decidedly changed atmosphere and Lenechka was quickly back to his original obnoxious self, demanding why it had taken this much time to tell him.

Maybe it's because of this attitude of yours, protested Parveen. Do you need reminding we are all Facilitators with one mission, to find out what the Presence is and how the hell the ^{235}U is appearing and disappearing.

Let's not forget this is weapons grade stuff. In the wrong hands it would be catastrophic, especially with every Zone on class 1 alert.

We just can't work out if there is any link between the ^{235}U and the Presence, but if not, what a coincidence.

So stop showing us your Russian arrogance and apply your mind to the problem, they implored Lenechka.

Another question Lenechka, pursued Dhul Fiqaar, why did you respond by only asking if we had any direct experience of the force field. You were the only Facilitator from hundreds who asked such a question. Explanation please ?

Not overly blessed with subtlety, Lenechka dropped his stare, unfolded his arms and slumped into the chair. Easy, he sighed, "it is because I have sensed it too".

This and barrage of questions with repeated demands of, when? and where?

The detail was remarkable in similarity, one difference being that it was only Lenechka who experienced the Presence, though it had happened to him on three occasions. Once outside a nuclear power plant and twice at his home.

Nothing as disturbing as the shaking car incident but still leaving Lenechka with a feeling of dread and impotence. So frustrating that I could not tell anyone, he protested, not even my fellow Facilitators.

So you can now maybe understand why I have been overly cautious with you all.

This revelation was so badly needed to start the process of complete problem sharing.

So wrapped up in their own world, these five Facilitators had forgotten the tensions across the world in all Zones. Fuelled by distrust and ignorance regarding the ^{235}U and the inexplicable movement of the material.

Patience had run out from many Zone leaders and the five were to be joined by other Facilitators from Zone 001 (USA), Zones 049 (France) and Zone 131 (Germany). These extra Facilitators to be expected within a few days.

Hurt pride, anger and frustration all combined to make the five even more impotent. It is turning into a bloody tea party they complained but what else could their leaders do.

Communications had been reduced to SMS messages between the Zones and the Facilitators as they waited helplessly for the new arrivals.

If they arrive and we are still seen as incompetents then not only will the potential global problem further deteriorate but the fact that they are here will reflect very badly on each of us, observed Monique. Always mindful of the perception games people play, particularly politicians and Zone leaders.

We must have some form of plan even a shaky strategy that makes their attendance useless, unless, commented Aaheru, they really can make a contribution and our pride blocks that.

The fact that other Facilitators were due galvanised Lenechka, and at long last he was becoming a team player.

Firstly he wanted to see the illegal ^{235}U held at the local al-Dabaa plant and then seek confirmation of the material held in the other eight Zones. He was justifiably cynical and wanted proof before he became further involved.

Then he wanted to rationalise why there seemed to be a correlation between the Presence and the illegal ^{235}U. For as convincing as everyone sounded, there really was an acute lack of objective evidence, just mindless speculation he reasoned, which is just not good enough !

It was true that when questioned objectively, not one of the Facilitators could provide any evidence.

In fact they argued the unquestionable manifestation of the Presence was in itself reason to consider a relationship with the transient movement of the ^{235}U.

As both occurred at nearly the same time and more importantly, the same place.

So, have there been any contacts with the Presence in

India	093
Bangladesh	076
Philippines	059
Vietnam	128
Sri Lanka	111
Nigeria.	067
Pakistan.	132
Indonesia.	099

the Zones who have intercepted illegal ^{235}U.

Parveen, Monique, Dhul Fiqaar, Aaheru could only reply that their call to all Facilitators regarding any force filed experiences was their coded request, with the same question.

Indeed, as evidenced by the fact that he was standing there asking these questions, Lenechka was the only Facilitator to respond with anything positive.

Was their subtlety the reason only Lenechka replied. Could it be that other Facilitators had experienced the Presence but felt too embarrassed to admit it. Or simply did not make a connection between their requests for a force field feedback, and the Presence.

All five were reluctant to open these questions up to a wider audience and concluded somewhat arbitrarily that if the Presence had been experienced somewhere else that it makes no difference to their dilemma, here.

If they are unable to make a positive link then maybe they should speculate a theorem and seek, not construct, evidence to support it.

This they did, and it was the turning point in this frustrating enigma.

Brainstorming many options they finally settled on the idea that the Presence was either warning mankind or threatening him. Quite why either theory applied, they could not defend. But they concluded,

Mankind was being given, one last chance.

But at last they had reasoned a causal link which gave them confidence and ambition to pursue this theory rigorously.

The theory became wild and exciting. They spent so many hours together that sleep and sustenance had to be forced upon the by their bodyguards, who were totally perplexed why their Facilitators were locked away in secrecy, day after day.

The American, French and Germany Facilitators arrived, as planned. This made the whole situation bloody near impossible.

Now Lenechka, Parveen, Monique, Dhul Fiqaar and Aaheru were running parallel routines. Their own, and the sham for the other three Facilitators who they fobbed off by directing them to double check on all of the work Parveen, Monique, Dhul Fiqaar and Aaheru had initially covered.

This can only last for so long they acknowledged, but maybe long enough for them to advance the dire theory.

Why would the Presence threaten mankind, by the manipulation of the ^{235}U. For all this did was to set mankind on a war footing, playing to his bigotry and prejudices. Man's ignorance had already force the planet into militarised Zones with Armageddon, a daily threat.

They challenged themselves to stop applying human logic and reason, for this was a presumptuous application which may well not apply to the Presence.

But if not this logic, then what common denominator could be applied.

For if they stumbled inadvertently through a serendipitous mistake to reach the Presence's communication portal, then surely that must be a level of success.

Again presumption. What if their conclusion or suggestion was at variance to what the Presence wanted or intended. Could this cause alienation or rejection.

Again they were assuming the Presence had an agenda else why it would threaten mankind.

And if it is a threat, then what consequences would mankind face for continuing on the same perilous path. A threat has to be made to be taken seriously, not implied or suggested. So what was the reason for terrifying four Facilitators stranded in the middle of the desert, in a freezing cold car.

What utter bollocks ! protested Dhul Fiqaar

This is getting us absolutely nowhere. We are playing infantile games and I for one am getting pretty well fed up with it, he exclaimed.

Presence, what bloody Presence. It's all a figment of our collective imaginations, he continued to ramble. But his protestations fell on deaf ears, for the other four had the bit between their teeth and were determined to develop their theories.

If you are that burnt out and cannot contribute Dhul Fiqaar, then we suggest you leave and retire for the night. We love you our friend, but this is too serious for childish antics and tantrums.

Join in, seriously contribute, or leave us alone.

This rebuffal really hurt Dhul Fiqaar who looked sheepish and isolated. His crestfallen look was all the apologies they needed. A hand shake and warm embrace had the five working together in minutes.

So a threat, how would this be delivered, particularly to a global audience. Or are the messengers, we five.

The chosen ones, the disciples, no that's not appropriate, the messengers is as grand as our title should be. Yet they knew they needed something quite remarkable to even begin to influence the Zone leaders that they are under notice. A threat notice.

If a threat, was the Presence trying to make mankind change his ways and become more conciliatory and open to compromise and reason.

That would be one hell of a 'mountain to climb', after centuries of war and isolationism.

If mankind tried to dismantle the Zonal status of the globe, then what would the resulting arrangements be.

A return to first, second and third would countries, with 50% of the planets populations unable to feed themselves, whilst still breeding like mindless rabbits.

The Zones were formed precisely because mankind could not or would not co-exist. Territorial gains, control of fossil based products, drinkable natural or water purification plants, precious natural minerals and not forgetting, old fashioned greed. Christ ! mankind really was and still is, a sick selfish animal.

And we are assuming the Presence wants this reversed, or else. Or else what. Mankind is doomed anyway. He has had the run of this planet, fucked it up and now it has to end.

So a possible if not probable doomsdays scenario that if the world did not change, it would be ended.

Let us take this thought on then, insisted Parveen. The Presence wants the world to back up a bit, a lot, whatever. It wants us to change, but into what and why, assuming reason was a part of the formula.

Does the Presence want to save mankind and if so, why. Does this nondescript energy field have some vested interest, a reason or need for the world to continue.

And what does to continue mean? With or without humans, or any life form?

Good point, if mankind messes up this planet, and perishes, but the planet as an inanimate object continues, then what would the Presence be left with.

A spinning mass of radio-active materials, substances, elements, compounds and any organisms that can survive irradiation.

The more they hypothesised and speculated the less clear why threatening mankind, would make sense.

Because of the intransient nature of man a warning, no matter how given would be ignored, that's for sure. So a threat. If the world doesn't change then it will end, be ended, whatever.

If this is the case then the manifestation of the illegal packages of ^{235}U would most certainly focus the mind of the Zone leaders. But, quickly added Monique, not in it's present form.

It may well be weapons grade uranium but there is no way, as it is, can constitute a threat.

If the Presence can move this material around and have it enriched then can it have the ^{235}U packaged into a nuclear bomb. Not just could it, but would it.

They were certainly swimming in the realms of wild fantasy now. But they agreed, without proof that the ^{235}U and the Presence were a pair, inter dependent and needing a solution for both, unless that is, if they can communicate with the Presence.

Full bloody circle screamed Aaheru. Can we just leave it there for now, this is ridiculous.

That evening over dinner the American, French and German Facilitators expressed their disquiet at being given redundant and demeaning tasks. They wanted to know what Lenechka, Parveen, Monique, Dhul Fiqaar, Aaheru had been up to these past few days.

The waffle that followed only angered the visitors who threatened to contact their masters to lodge a formal complaint. Suit yourself retorted Lenechka. Underlining that there was still no love lost between the Russians and the Yanks then, even after all these years.

Capitalism and Communism ideologies and practicalities. Ne'er the twain shall meet.

There was no real animosity between them, in fact they hardly knew anything about each other, but the Presence and ^{235}U problem was consuming them and the visitors were a distraction. Sooner they go, the better, was the considered view.

That included the fact that they had contributed nothing, which of course was precisely the intent.

An acrimonious send off followed as they flew back to Zones 001, 049 and 131.

There'll be hell to pay for this they agreed when those three report to their superiors. But that was for another time. Not today.

Bigger fish to fry. A world to save from itself.

Chapter 9.
The Beijing hostages.

Certainly Zone leaders were in continuous contact with each other, but only with a steady flow of trivia that masked their real uncertainties and fears of conspiracy and intrigue.

It would be naive to think that during the lead up to the Beijing summit that Zone leaders would idly sit back, leaving everything to the Facilitators. Nothing could be further from the truth.

Many had secretly communicated concerns and suspicions that a conspiracy plan was being realised. By whom and for what reason, that was their dilemma.

The very secrecy they suspected, would be their next strategy. Several Zones entrusted their Facilitator training specialists to conduct ruthless investigations into any clandestine organisation, who could arrange the ^{235}U manipulation.

Who would have such power, influence and authority to make this happen, completely unnoticed in eight Zones simultaneously. Even having the ability to dumbfound and confuse the Facilitators. No easy task. So who ?

The history databases provided a wealth of information on ostensively secretive organisations.

With the fragmentation of the world into 147 Zones many politicians, financiers, religious leaders and business people condemned what had happened.

But their protests had no formal forum and so what choice did they have but to take the 'broken law', into their own hands. Mankind had always been his own worst enemy, even when on the same side.

Facilitator training specialists from Russia, China, USA, France and the UK met in Rome, to pool their collective knowledge and wisdom into solving this mystery.

They started by listing the most likely of the 'known' so-called secret societies to establish who would have the influence to manage such a feat.

It took little time to track down and compromise members of every listed organisation, especially considering the powers these investigators had.

The pressures they forced upon their victims was totally uncompromising and was not restricted to the minions of each secret organisation.

Within a few days they had the details of the most senior people in each organisation. And here's where the real problems arose, for many of the world's most powerful people were implicated.

This included Zone leaders, of the highest order.

This caused the investigators to back-off until clear authorisation was given for specific actions to be taken.

Abduction and interrogation had topped their list but you cannot torture a King, President, or Head of Church. It had also identified that some of their own Ministers and department heads were directly involved.

This had become a major and embarrassing problem.

The investigators listed seventeen secret organisations who historically had or still have enough power and wealth to manage the ^{235}U threat.

How to attach the question of motive when investigating these organisations was from the outset extremely subjective and highly controversial.

In descending priority of potential threat these were:-

1. The Club

Super-exclusive - lord chancellors and bishops have been blackballed during its quarter century history - it comprises just fifty individuals, all male.

Mostly senior politicians, academics, financiers and members of the great and good, they meet one Tuesday each month in a private dining room off Piccadilly. UK.

2. The Weathermen

Espousing left-wing politics, they thrived in the 1970s and members declared themselves to be at war with the United States government. This included bombings.

Keen to see the destruction of US imperialism and the establishment of a classless, i.e. communist, world, the society allegedly disintegrated post Vietnam.

3. Nine Unknown Men.

No one has yet managed to produce any evidence proving the existence of this tiny group of individuals who 'really' run the world (let alone who they might be). But for believers that is all the proof they need to demonstrate the awesome power and omnipotence of the individuals in question.

Somewhat similar is the fabled Great White Lodge, which is said to have been founded by the ancient Egyptians - or possibly the Tribes of Israel. Its members also run the world, by directing other secret organisations such as the Freemasons, Knights Templar's and Illuminati.

4. The 33rd Degree .

A brass plaque on the wall at 10 Duke Street, London SW1, boldly identifies the Headquarters of the Supreme Council of the 33rd Degree, the higher echelons of the Masonic movement. Allegedly so secret that most Freemasons did not realise there were more than three degrees or levels to their craft. In fact, headed by a Most Puissant Sovereign

Commander, only 75 members can be 33rd Degree at one time, ensuring its exclusivity.

5. The Illuminati

or Perfectibilists. That existed in Upper Bavaria in the 1760s. At the time, members presented themselves as an order of enlightened free thinkers. and they came to be regarded by many as an underground force of dissidents intent on overthrowing the government.

The Illuminati have continued directing world industry and politics as it sees fit. With many prominent members, but no legitimate evidence of such a group has ever been uncovered. Expressly anti-religious, the chief aim is to create a new One World Government.

6. The Priory of Sion

Was apparently founded at some point between AD 20 and 1956. Its origins are French, and its principal objective concerned the establishment of a new dynasty of pan-European rulers.

These were to be united by a secret bloodline from France's Merovingian kings, the 6th- to 8th-century dynasty which some claim was descended from the offspring of Jesus and Mary Magdalene. Belief in the Priory's existence remains particularly strong.

7. The Black Hand:

Was a secret society of anti-imperialist political revolutionaries started in Serbia in 1912. It formed as an offshoot from Narodna Adbrona, a group that sought to unite all of the Slavic people of Europe under one country. The group began disseminating anti-Austrian propaganda and training saboteurs and assassins to disrupt political rule within the province.

Their plan was to incite war between Serbia and Austria, which would free their country and unite the different Slavic nations.

8. Bilderberg group

A secret society with no members but an impressive guest list, the Bilderberg is a sort of über-Davos, an annual summit of leading figures from the worlds of finance, politics, the military and media. With no press coverage, and positively no spectators, it has proved a gift for conspiracy theorists everywhere.

It was founded in 1956, chiefly to combat anti-Americanism in Europe and to keep alive the spark of Atlanticism that had been fired by allied cooperation in the second world war. To this end the closed nature of the meetings, says the committee, is merely intended to allow participants to speak openly and freely.

9. Ordo Templi Orientis:

General philosophy was a belief in new age esoteric principles and practices as a method of realizing one's true identity. No political agenda. It is an Outer Thelemic Order dedicated to the high purpose of securing the Liberty of the Individual and his or her advancement in Light, Wisdom, Understanding, Knowledge and Power. This is accomplished through Beauty, Courage and Wit, on the Foundation of Universal Brotherhood.

10. The Thule Society:

The group was unofficially started in Germany just after the end of WWI. It began as a kind of German heritage group that dabbled in the occult, but it quickly transformed into an organization that sought to forward the ideology of the Aryan race, and it took an outwardly racist approach toward Jews and other minorities.

11. Skull and Bones:

Skull and Bones counts among its membership U.S. Presidents, Senators, and Supreme Court Justices, which has lead many to argue that the group works as some kind of underground organization for the high-powered political elite.

There is no denying that the club is well funded: Unusually, for its first century and a half, it made no secret of its membership, and lists of names were routinely filed at the university's library. However, that stopped in the early 1970s.

12. The Freemasons

Officially founded in 1717, but documents relating to its existence date back to the 1300s. It was originally created to be a brotherhood whose members share certain key philosophical ideas, among them a belief in a supreme being. The group stresses moral uprightness, and as such many of the chapters have become known for their charitable work and community service.

13. **Opus Dei**

Established in Spain by St Josemaría Escrivá in 1928, Opus Dei is perhaps more secretive than secret - not least because the Catholic Church, of which it is a part, formally banned secret societies many years ago. It teaches that ordinary life is a path to sanctity. It is, even so, dogged with controversy. Critics say it is elitist, dangerously right-wing and misogynistic, whilst the practice by some celibate members of self-flagellation (or mortification of the flesh) is considered distasteful.

14. **ODESSA**

The German Organisation for Former SS Members. In particular the group organised and maintained so-called ratlines or escape routes, enabling SS members to flee Germany following defeat, giving new lives for themselves and their families in South America.

It is thought to have helped at least ten thousand officers and men to escape in this way.

The burning ambition to once again seek power, is fact.

15. **The Sons of Liberty:**

existed in America prior to the Revolutionary War. The group was made up of smaller factions of patriots from across the colonies that united in support of a common goal. The group would meet in Boston around the Liberty Tree. It was here that the group would formulate their resistance, which included the dissemination of pamphlets and even some sabotage and terrorist activity.

16. The Knights of the Golden Circle:

Flourished in the U.S. during the American Civil War. In the beginning, the group sought to encourage the annexation of Mexico and the West Indies, which they believed would help the waning slave trade to once again flourish. But once the Civil War started, the group switched its focus from colonialism to fervent support of the newly established Confederate government. The Knights soon had thousands of followers, many of whom formed guerilla armies and began raiding Union strongholds in the West. In the Northern states, the mysterious order had an even bigger impact.

17. Hashshashin– The Order of Assassins:

These were Muslim assassins operating in the Middle East during the 13th century. The group was made up of Shia Muslims leaving a larger sect in order to establish a utopian Shi'ite state. The group used guerilla tactics in their battles including espionage, sabotage, and, most famously, political assassination. The would plant highly trained moles inside enemy strongholds, with instructions to only attack when the time was right.

Not surprisingly the whole investigation was dropped as the list of dignitaries and highly influential people grew, including those supposedly promoting and authorising the investigation.

It was clearly untenable and with increasing concern and intervention, all investigations ceased with instructions to physically destroy any and all records.

One Frenchman even suggested asking these organisations if they could help in the ^{235}U problem. Knowing when to stop asking, is a career choice.

The main rebuffal came from those most protective of their own secrecy and privacy. Those arguably with most to lose would shout the loudest and yet the quiet ones would go seemingly unnoticed.

Surely, scoffed many, whoever is behind this mystery are so clandestine that they will never leave themselves open to discovery.

Suicide and murder were no longer bygone principles designed to keep very private matters, that way.

Step out of line in any Zone and severe repercussions would follow, not just affecting the individual, but their families and working colleagues.

This uncompromising code of conduct was felt even more necessary with the forming of the 147 Zones.

When there is unrest and instability, people must know who they can trust, even people they do not like.

Dedication to a cause, can force many odd bedfellows.

It was not long before the aborted investigation of secret organisations became public knowledge and the societal paranoia just increased exponentially.

The ^{235}U fiasco was becoming too well known across many Zones, not the detail, for nobody had that, but the fact that Zone ministries were investigating paranormal events, in numerous Zones.

That alone was enough to fuel speculation and further distrust, placing many Zones onto a war footing.

The next round of meetings in Beijing had been called for the 18th August 2060 and was scheduled to last for five days, subject to developments. Senior representatives from every Zone were invited, along with their entourages.

What was obvious this time, though in non military clothing, were the military generals and advisors.

This was more like a war council that a peace seeking forum. Many of the Zones had commenced tactical war games and training manoeuvres which included flying bombers and fighters around their air spaces. Posturing and brinkmanship at its worst.

Like testosterone loaded teenagers they strut around emulating eunuchs, in a pathetic display of arrogant body language. It is a characteristic of people in command to try to emit a aura of superiority and indifference. This is the last things needed at this time.

Is it any wonder the world is so fucked up. Mankind has developed in so many ways and yet regressed in many others, like Neanderthals in uniforms, sauntering about wearing costumes of high office.

If it truly is the intention of the Presence to threaten mankind then what will it take from a force field, unable or unwilling to communicate, to have any impact on these Zone leaders.

They continued to meet but one day came news that the eight packages of illegal ^{235}U had once again disappeared.

Through the summit chairman all Zones agree to instruct their Ministries to expedite detailed investigations of all nuclear power plants and storage facilities to see if once again the packages had materialised.

Many leaders advocated disbanding the summit, but for what. If they all returned to their Zones then isolationism would prevail, which would once again fuel speculation that other Zones were planning strategic strikes, or that terrorists were master minding attacks.

For goodness sake maintain calm and reason, beseeched the summit chairman. We must stay close to each other and fully co-ordinate any plans and agreements.

A motion was passed that if any Zones were in collusion, or in any way instrumental in these games of psychological warfare with the illegal ^{235}U, then a terrible retribution would be visited upon them.

To threaten terrorists, if indeed they were behind this, was futile.

The usual mix of political doves and hawks were of a single mind to end this nightmarish situation as soon as possible. But no one seemed to ask why it was lasting for so long including the impotency of their Facilitators.

Their judgement was clouded by frustration and fear. Rational thinking was simply not there.

Their worse fears were realised when reports came in that the illegal packages of ^{235}U had reappeared as complete Gun-triggered Fission nuclear bombs.

The technical experts in the entourages updated their political masters on what this meant. So how does it work ? was the most immediate question.

A sphere of ^{235}U is made around the neutron generator and a small bullet of ^{235}U is removed. The bullet is placed at the one end of a long tube with explosives behind it, while the sphere is placed at the other end.

The explosives fire and propel the bullet down the barrel. The bullet strikes the sphere and generator, initiating the fission reaction. The fission reaction begins. The bomb explodes.

However the problems became exponential when the reports also stated that very sophisticated anti tamper devices had been attached to each bomb.

As the core uranium could now not be directly accessed and therefore confirmed as the same batch of the illegal ^{235}U, it had to be accepted as the same.

If just one of these bombs were to be detonated then chaos would ensue.

Even early nuclear fission bombs were thousands of times more explosive than a comparable mass of chemical explosive.

For example, Little Boy atomic bomb (August 1945) weighed a total of four tons, of which 60 kg was nuclear fuel, just 3.4 m long; and yielded an explosion equivalent to about 15 kilotons of TNT, destroying most of the city of Hiroshima.

Modern nuclear weapons, which include a thermonuclear fusion as well as one or more fission stages, are literally hundreds of times more energetic for their weight than the first pure fission atomic bombs.

So that a modern single missile warhead bomb weighing less than seven kilograms has a yield of 475,000 tons of TNT, and could bring destruction to a massive city area.

The 2½ kilograms of ^{235}U in each package would have a devastating impact. This would trigger totally irrational retaliatory responses, then the domino effect and all out thermal nuclear global war.

Not really a war for no one would be targeting a particular Zone for reason of confrontation, it would be mindless, irrational, indiscriminate global destruction.

In 2018 NATO had completed phase three of the powerful X-band radar missile defence system that protected the territories of all NATO member states in Europe and North America.

It was capable of intercepting long-range missiles fired from the Middle East.

The United States had also collaborated with Israel and friendly Persian Gulf nations to establish and improve their antimissile abilities.

That had been preceded when the USA military established a radar facility in Israel and much to everyone's surprise did the same in nearby Arab nations. The main reason being the vital early alarm of any potential missile firings from Iran, thus increasing the chances of intercepting the weapons.

The US President Obama administration (2008 – 2012) had started the deployment of 436 SM-3 interceptors around the world which was completed in 2016.

This pre-occupation with defence most certainly contributed to the isolationism attitude that led to the formation of the Zones.

These reminders of modern history taunted the Zone leaders at the Beijing summit. Could nothing be learned from past experiences. But one thing to have these nightmares return to haunt, but there has to be the desire and willingness to compromise and to take a risk.

Most politicians and diplomats were very willing to open global reintegration talks, but the military said absolutely no. So a stalemate, as it was argued that such was the infrastructure in every Zone, that a reconciliation any level was militarily impractical.

And why, why bother, many argued. It will only be a matter of time before mankind increases the populations without any care for provisions to sustain and support such growth. Then back to square one. The full circle.

We are simply not meant to survive as a species. This feeling was held by so many and clearly formed the majority view. But and as always, these Zone leaders did not want to die.

They had families, the trappings of office, wealth and power. And the prospect of slowly dying from radiation, if not annihilated with half a second of a detonation, was unconscionable.

Back to the real time problem of the fully armed and primed thermal nuclear devices that could not be defused, led to a barrage of ideas. The most popular of which was to detonate each device underground.

But the testing caverns used many years ago were no longer accessible.

Besides there are anti tamper devices attached to each bomb. So how sophisticated could these systems be.

To their horror the found out that each bomb had a GPS co-ordinate tolerance of no more that 5 metres.

Put simply, Move the bomb away from its present resting place and it will detonate. They tried shielding the bomb so that any form of GPS radio wave uplink would be blocked and the bomb primed, starting a countdown. Remove the shield and it stopped. Seems it needs to talk to the three satellites that give tri-angulation location. It had thermal sensitive and movement detection circuits.

Can't move it, or defuse it, so what the bloody hell is going on. What are we to do. And then another realisation.

The location of the bombs fell into a cross stream of weather patterns, jet steams and thermal cyclones. It took little time to calculate that if these bombs detonated that the radioactive fallout would cover over 80% of the globe within 24 hours.

Survival raced through everyone's mind.

But for goodness sake, common sense told them they wouldn't survive, well not for long, in any event. Even if they reached their Zones and burrowed underground into their fallout shelters. How long could they stay there.

Even with this awful fact staring them in the face several delegates decided to leave the summit.

As the first returned to their hotels, packed and went to their limousines; the call went out. The bombs had primed again and started a countdown. But this is absolutely impossible they shrieked. A fucking mechanical bomb that is aware of individuals movements.

Completely confused all delegates returned to the hotel complexes, then the summit hall. Within minutes the bombs stopped the countdown, back into standby mode.

These eight thermal nuclear bombs had literally taken every Zone leader hostage in Beijing. How the hell is that possible and did it apply to all members of the entourage. It did not, for several junior staff members secreted themselves to the airports and back home. The bombs remained in standby mode.

So those inconsequential staff did not feature in the grand order of things, only the senior politicians and military chiefs had any role in this incredible situation.

Did the bombs have a voice recognition system, as daft as that sounded could these devices be spoken to, reasoned with. Could negotiations take place, could a compromise be reached, a settlement.

This was absolutely ridiculous and brought scorn and ridicule from many.

For so three days all delegates met in the summit hall and talked and talked but not a single idea or solution was forthcoming. Just frustrated and pitiful old men and women prattling on like verbose cretins.

Unbeknown to the delegates the five Facilitators had arrived in Beijing, in fact on the 19th August but stayed on the outskirts of Beijing, in Mentougou.

Close enough to visit the summit if called but far enough away to remain undetected.

So what were they hoping to achieve, that's if they had a plan or were they just in reaction mode.

Remember that so far they were the only ones to know of the Presence. Would they share this unsubstantiated knowledge, more belief, even conviction, to their illustrious leaders at the summit.

If they did what would be the response. Rejection no doubt, criticism, rebuffal, certainly sanctions.

Their gut feelings was to just return to their respective Zones and yet, and yet. Was this not as much their problem as it was the rest of the world, well those that knew what was going on.

So they decided to invite themselves to the summit.

Chapter 10.
Decision time.

Contact with their respective leaders brought scepticism and criticism. What are you doing here when you should be back in Zone 108 finding solutions, they were constantly asked.

The Russians were particularly angry that Lenechka had joined Parveen, Monique, Dhul Fiqaar and Aaheru in Zone 108 unbeknown to them. So what had he found out or contributed, and above all what had he said to the American who had joined them for those few days.

"Ебать от проклятого Ленечка" "Это все наши лидеры могут говорить и делать в такое время".

[Is this all our leaders can say and do at a time like this.]

Seems all nationalities have the same basic problems between leaders and their followers.

The angry outbursts over, the five were told to report to the summit hall the following day, at 9am.

That night in Mentougou the five soul searched. Went through more scenarios than is sensible and just ended up arguing and contradicting each other. Alcohol played an important part in distraction and relaxation.

A light supper, then to bed. Hoping for sleep was more than a little naive and each hour lasted a lifetime as they laid waiting for the Presence to put in an appearance.

Not to be. Like some bloody circus ringmaster it would orchestrate it's grand appearance at some totally unexpected and unsuitable time and place. If it did, would they really be the only five people to sense the Presence, surely not and if not, what would follow. Panic, hysteria, aggression ?

Ten tired and sore eyes instinctively found their way to the breakfast room. Little conversation, more a series of self pitying moans and an agreement to meet in reception at 8am.

To keep the numbers at a sensible level only one bodyguard would be needed per Facilitator.

A thirty minute drive and the summit hall loomed dauntingly large and foreboding. With the many stone steps leading to the entrance, flanked by heavily armed guards. The integral security scanners identified each as a Facilitator, as the heavy, bullet proof doors swung open into a vast foyer, with towering marble pillars.

They were tannoyed to report to their respective Zone leaders meeting rooms. But refused. No, we will not be separated they protested.. We must stay together at all times. No divide and conquer.

This bought mixed reactions from their superiors. Two ordered security guards to arrest the Facilitators but as the guards advanced the Facilitators stood their ground and warned the security guards to back off, remember who we are, they shouted,

"We are Facilitators, you do not touch us, ever !"

Followed a shouting match between Zone leaders and the Facilitators, the guards backed off, particularly when the bodyguards appeared on the scene. These people you do not mix with, for they have a terrifying reputation for no compromise and a total dedication.

The five sets of Zone leaders acquiesced and started talking in compromising terms.

Lenechka, Parveen, Monique, Dhul Fiqaar and Aaheru had taken a terrible risk in their stance but absolutely could not see any other way forward.

They made it very clear to their superiors that they would remain as one. They insisted in being allowed to function and operate together in every respect.

وسوف المسيل للدموع قطعنا إلى عند امدعن انل قطع لقق عودن إلى من انطقنا

[They will tear us to pieces when we return];thought Dhul Fiqaar. But that's for another day.

The Facilitators asked if they could address the Zone Leaders in the summit hall, again insisting they remain together at all times. All five on the podium , talking to over a thousand of the worlds most influential people.

What could they say, at this vitally critical time.

They decided to distract the delegates with talk of the International Space Station (ISS) launched in 2000 as the largest human-made object ever to orbit the Earth. An engineering feat still unsurpassed in 2060.

The reason for this distraction was to lead the delegates thinking into the possibility of the ISS being a launch platform that somehow contributed to the eight thermal nuclear bombs. No matter how implausible.

How it had been utilised would further fuel the delegates imagination, it was hoped. It had regular visits by space shuttle, to resupply and add new modules. The ISS was operated by the Expedition 22 crew, consisting two from USA's NASA, two from Russia's RKA, and one from Japan's JAXA.

Since the initial launch of the ISS literally hundreds had visited from many Zones. Some for extended stays and if so, then what were they actually doing up there all that time. The Facilitators were winding up the conspiracy theory but not really getting the inter-action with the delegates they were hoping for.

Even mention of the ISS size and capabilities failed to impress the delegates.

The ISS measures 357 feet end-to-end Solar Array Length: 239.4 feet weighing one million pounds.

The 84 kilowatts of average power for the ISS is supplied by an acre of solar panels

The 55-foot robot arm assembly is capable of lifting 220,000 pounds.

The station is maintained at an orbit between 278 km and 460 km altitude, and travels at an average speed of 27,743.8 km/h completing 15.7 orbits per day.

The ISS was supposedly de-commissioned in 2034 after a series of accidents whilst installing a radio telescope close to the visual telescope.

More distraction when they told the delegates that the Star Wars near-space laser defence systems had been built, developed and tested from the ISS.

The ISS had apparently launched metal debris out to space away from the earth then tracked and destroyed these targets using the lasers. If this is true, then maybe not so benign after all.

Could, speculated the Facilitators, could the ISS be implicated in some way.

Amidst critical cross examination by the delegates Lenechka protested, lets us not be too quick to dismiss the ISS. Did the ISS not have technical laboratories with stores of space proof materials with earth re-entry capabilities.

What the Americans, Russians and Japanese did up there for year after year has always been a closely kept secret. What was reported was almost certainly misinformation, designed to mislead or confuse. Who, other than those who had visited the ISS, could possibly comment, and then how much would be the truth.

Also when was the last visitor to the ISS. The only way to gain access to the ISS was through the Space Shuttle programme. Though it is true the shuttle technology was widely available to any nation with the finances and resources, from 2015 onwards. That gave nineteen years for ISS manned projects before the ISS was 'allegedly' closed down. If indeed it has been closed down.

But this speculation was really just another distraction, it had to be, surely they reasoned. And even though there was a consensus to not pursue the ISS question, it was still a niggling thought.

Returning to the summit hall and their request to address the delegates.

Monique, Lenechka, Aaheru, Parveen and Dhul Fiqaar, needed to be as certain as they could, that their proclamations were plausible and that the Zone leaders were hearing something they wanted to hear. No more uncertainty or confusion. Not more upsets or bad news. Give them something reassuring or this game of psychology will surely backfire.

First question. Will the Facilitators be hoping to de-escalate the tensions that have been building since the first appearance of the ^{235}U and finally the nuclear bombs. Bombs that somehow seemed to have an intelligence of their own.

Inanimate devices that can sense the physical movement of Zone leaders when attempting to leave the confines of the summit hall. These bombs could arm then disarm at will whilst located hundreds of miles apart.

Did the Presence have a role to play here and if so, what. They kept needing to remind themselves that only they had direct personal experience of the Presence.

Equally the Presence had never made any reference to the bombs or anything else, even indirectly, so surely that must be discounted. It was they who had made the implausible link out of desperation.

What to say, how to say it.

Okay lets start by reminding them of the worse case scenario. That being some idiot panics and detonates a nuclear device, for if that were to happen then the world would surely come to an end.

So that is not an option for any rational person. We cannot cater for the irrational and so will not waste time contemplating how they could be managed.

So the argument at this stage is one of survival. If the planet survives for another year, a decade or an indeterminate time. Would having time, facilitate compromise and meaningful progress, and if so to what agenda. The worlds population had certainly not decreased to a level where crop yield, fishing and farming could support the human race.

Even with genetically modified food production the worlds population would explode within a decade and be totally unsustainable.

Many argued that survival of the fittest or more accurately natural selection must then be the only possible, solution.

Herbert Spencer first used the phrase — after reading Charles Darwin's, 'On the Origin of Species', in his Principles of Biology (1864), in which he drew parallels between his own economic theories and Darwin's biological ones, writing "This survival of the fittest, when expressed in mechanical terms, is that which Mr. Darwin has called 'natural selection', or the preservation of favoured races in the struggle for life."

Darwin first used Herbert Spencer's phrase "survival of the fittest" as a synonym for "natural selection" in the fifth edition of On the Origin of Species, published in 1869. Darwin meant it as a metaphor for "better adapted for immediate, local environment", not the common inference of "in the best physical shape". Hence, it is not a scientific description.

The phrase "survival of the fittest" is not generally used by modern biologists as the term does not accurately convey the meaning of natural selection, the term biologists use and prefer. Natural selection refers to differential reproduction as a function of traits that have a genetic basis.

"Survival of the fittest" is inaccurate for two important reasons. First, survival is merely a normal prerequisite to reproduction. Second, fitness has specialized meaning in biology, different from how the word is used in popular culture. In population genetics, fitness refers to differential reproduction.

"Fitness" does not refer to whether an individual is physically fit, bigger, faster or stronger, or better in any subjective sense. It refers to a difference in reproductive rate from one generation to the next.

An interpretation of the phrase "survival of the fittest" to mean "only the fittest organisms will prevail" is not consistent with the actual theory of evolution. Any individual organism which succeeds in reproducing itself is "fit" and will contribute to survival of its species, not just the "physically fittest" ones. Though some of the population will be better adapted to the circumstances, than others.

A more accurate characterisation of evolution would be "survival of the fit enough". This is also emphasised by the fact that while direct competition has been observed between individuals, populations and species, there is little evidence that competition has been the driving force in the evolution of large groups.

As seen between amphibians, reptiles and mammals; rather these animals have evolved by expanding into empty ecological niches.

Moreover, to misunderstand or misapply the phrase to simply mean "survival of those who are better equipped for surviving" is rhetorical tautology. What Darwin meant was "better adapted for immediate, local environment" by differential preservation of organisms that are better adapted to live in changing environments.

The concept is not tautological, as it contains an independent criterion of fitness.

These periods of research are characteristic of how Facilitators work. But how can five isolated Facilitators stand in front of such an audience and promote the idea of enforced natural selection, for that is, in itself, a contradiction.

The eight nuclear bombs were only hostage takers not mechanised legislators, which obviously has to remain with the presently enslaved Zone leaders. And it is that fact that has to be laboured. Driven home to a point of stark realisation.

The inbred arrogance of mankind nearly always leads him to believe he has to be judge and jury. An ultimate decision making system, pouring contempt and scorn on anyone who happens to disagree.

So for this proposition to work strip mankind of that parochial attitude and have him operate in total vulnerability. Let him have no ability to make decisions but rather to come to terms with the inevitable.

So what is inevitable. The horrifying fact that mankind has to reduce its numbers and limit future breeding. This is the living nightmare and the Orwellian predicts of such a civilisation having to become a reality. Everything history had warned against. The countless wars and endless deaths, all to defend the right of people to live in freedom, which is now the very thing that is killing mankind.

They had their freedom and flagrantly abused it. Resulting in over population, endless wars, corruption and ravaging of the planet's natural resources, all conspired to sound the death knell. It was the bizarre idea of a slow but inevitable, mass suicide.

Then the possibility that the five Facilitators were not in fact disciples or instruments of doom, but survival. Could this be that their selection was as arbitrary as that. Was it fate, or some form of serendipity that chanced their being together, at this time, and is this way.

They were self indulging and fantasising but taking no comfort in either, for their fate was to become the messengers of the most terrible governance ever to be imposed on man.

The selective culling of mankind. Such an idea made the holocaust look pitifully insignificant.

Who, where, why and when. And how to explain their logic to the Zone leaders.

The exodus from the summit of the Zone leaders had stopped and the Nuclear bombs remained inert.

Resigned, they decided that limited extermination and future population control, would be their proposal, as indefensible as it might sound.

The ramifications in every Zone would be extreme when it became apparent that women were not becoming pregnant, though the realisation would take several months. This dilemma would be compounded when the elite in each Zone would refuse to be denied their right to breed.

The wealthy and influential would have families and the poor masses would not.

This course of action would have to be radical and should be planned to have a global reduction in population of 10% per annum until 50% reduction had been achieved.

This dramatic course of action was needed as so many wars had been territorial as populations wanted to increase their lands for crop growth and living accommodation. Often even minor cross border skirmishes would escalate into war, lasting for years.

So how would this be achieved. Firstly the Zone leaders had to accept unanimously the requirement for dramatic population reduction. This was simply, genocide.

Next, the essential follow up sterilisation of survivors.

The first option was surgical intervention to end fertility permanently. Traditionally this involved the removal or interruption of the anatomical pathways through which the cells involved in fertilisation, travel. The operations are vasectomy in men and tubal ligation in women.

Obvious disadvantages are forcing the people to volunteer, then the demands placed on hospitals, the cost and logistics and finally the social revolt this would bring. So surgical intervention had to be dismissed.

For men only, could be the progressive and discrete exposure to toxic chemicals or radiation. However this would also affect those members of society who would be allowed to have more children.

The effects of sexually transmitted diseases, cancer and cancer treatments were totally random and could not be calculated into any programme.

So, for population containment there seems to be but one option, that of abortifacient. This is a substance that induces abortion and includes mifepristone used with misoprostol. Pharmaceutical abortifacients prostaglandin analogues, such as misoprostol or gemeprost, are used to terminate advanced pregnancy, in combination with mifepristone (a progesterone receptor antagonist) or methotrexate (an antifolate).

There are also herbal mixtures e.g. bloodroot, mandrake, pennyroyal, yucca, and mistletoe all have very strong progesterone binding activity and are used as abortifacents to create an abortion, and bring on menses.

This option seems the least obvious or confrontational and would be administered by contaminating the water supplies, in literally every surviving Zone.

Large scale application had never been tried, so the quantities required and the methods of infecting the water supplies would be a logistic nightmare. But it had to be done.

This then would be the Facilitators message to the delegates. How would they react and would the eight nuclear bombs de-activate, to allow the delegate hostages unrestricted passage back to their Zones to put this dastardly plan into effect.

Lenechka, Parveen, Monique, Dhul Fiqaar and Aaheru had a stressful evening and very restless night.

Breakfast was a wasted farce as they wrestled with the day ahead and what might transpire.

Into one car and onto the steps of the summit hall. The sun shone defiantly with the occasional cloud scurrying by, least it block confidence giving ultra violet rays.

The Facilitators needed all the energy and confidence they could muster for the daunting tasks ahead as their fears transcended their own reputation.

If they had to argue the relative merits of their suggestion then all would be lost.

For the academics, philosophers, anti abortionists, pacifists and religious zealots would cause delay after delay and start doubt raising, protracted debates.

It would then never happen and the Zonal state would return with all the associated terrors.

They knew they could not mention the Presence, least they be branded delusional idiots.

Each of the many steps up to the entrance doors of the summit hall seemed interminable. They felt as if the eyes of everyone there were focussed on them. Arms interlinked they cleared the few remaining steps and walked up to the massive foreboding glass doors. Security did not need a second experience with the Facilitators especially with the now ten bodyguards in close attendance.

They walked through the magnificent foyer, with all those attending, stepping back to create a clear pathway into the summit hall. Like the biblical parting of the waves. Then they were inside the hall, staring down on hundreds of seats, rows of tables, chairs and an ocean of microphones and communication consoles.

They were breathing in concert as their hearts beat palpably. And these trembling wrecks were the most highly trained and skilled people on this troubled planet.

"This way",. called out a steward and gestured to the podium. Christ, they thought, we are the first on. Not even a 'warm up' act. As they made their way to the podium the delegates started flooding in with their minions and attendant staff.

It seemed a lifetime until the last of the delegates settled themselves in.

Then the chairman of the summit stood up and again welcomed all delegates.

Today, ladies and gentlemen, we have a totally unscripted programme, he proclaimed.

You do not need me to spell out the recent developments, most of which beggars belief. There are so many unanswered questions he continued. So much uncertainty, at a time when certainty is needed.

An entropy moment with out any doubt he reflected.

A measure of a leaders ability to lead is not when times are settled and those around are in compliant mode. It is when an unprecedented crises strikes, never seen before.

We are all Zone leaders and we quite literally have the future of this globe in our hands. The manifestation of the ^{235}U and now the eight nuclear bombs that seem almost to know what we think and feel and have taken us hostage, the chairman continued.

As you can see on the podium, we are joined today by the most powerful people our governments have ever trained and released onto the world. The Facilitators whose intellect and powers of deductive reasoning is unparalleled. So we must listen to them, he stressed.

By name they are Lenechka, Parveen, Monique, Dhul Fiqaar and Aaheru and they come from Zones 014 : 004 : 047 and 108: They have been involved with this problem from the very beginning and so we are hoping they can shed light on what has happened, where we are now and what to do next.

I urgently beseech you to listen very careful to what they have to say. Let them finish and do not interrupt or over-react. Like you, I do not know what they are going to say, but I intend to listen carefully, he concluded.

The summit hall fell into a strange, eerie, silence. The atmosphere tense, expectations high, the uncertainty vibrant. It is amazing how intimidating having an audience can be, as the five shuffled nervously. Who the hell was going to start, had not been thought through.

So Parveen stepped forward and nervously shouted into the microphone, stood back apologised, regained her composure and started again.

Delegates she called, we Facilitators have been created to police this fragmented world travelling between the 147 Zones, for the express purpose of detecting and eliminating any threat.

You have given us unlimited powers and in our years of existence the Facilitator programme has been very successful, with every threat or problem we have uncovered, having been resolved.

But this one, this one, she repeated, has been a complete enigma. The like of which has never been seen before and more importantly is a threat that affects the entire planet, not just one or two Zones, but everyone. From our investigations, we have come to a conclusion.

Sensing she had said enough she stepped back and ushered the other four Facilitators to take centre stage. Like a bashful but verbose Oscar winner, Dhul Fiqaar took up the story explaining the events in chronological order, inviting interjections from the others, as he sought to draw a meaningful picture.

For he knew, like the others, that the concluding recommendation would be a bombshell to the delegates.

As he progressed the telling of this mystery, coughing and clearing of throats echoed around the vast summit hall. The delegates were becoming restless, sensing that the situation had a bitter end.

The chairman called for a steadying calm. Please delegates, please let them finish.

The moment had come, the words had to be spoken and in almost one voice Lenechka, Parveen, Monique, Dhul Fiqaar and Aaheru declared:-

We must reduce the worlds population by 50%, in order to survive, that coupled with severe population control.

An incredible silence followed, so loud, it was deafening. The only disturbance was the sharp intake of breath from the delegates.

Further silence with looks of utter disbelief and incredulity etched on their faces.

It didn't seem possible but the Facilitators had been talking for over an hour and their statements and explanations had been immaculately and convincingly articulated.

Their energy tempered with pragmatism and logic was flawless and the delegates were left without reason, justification or cause, to revolt and reject.

A few minutes passed as the entire summit tried to collect their thoughts, when suddenly there was a deafening sound of mobile telephones and intercoms screaming into life.

The eight nuclear bombs had re-armed and were on countdown. This incredible phenomenon caused further consternation as the chorus of telephones came to a restful, silent state.

The summit chairman stood up clearly alarmed and distressed, as the ripples of disbelief and shock subsided and the ringtones faded.

Though something that had been at the back of many people's mind for years, it was unimaginable that one day the actually question would be asked and more importantly, an answer given.

No procrastination, no waffle, no protests, just the awful realisation that it, or something very close to it, would have to happen and soon.

The chairman suggested a break in proceedings for time to absorb and think through what was being proposed. He told the delegates to reconvene that afternoon at 4pm. At which time he added soberly, we will have to make a decision.

He had no idea if the eight nuclear bombs on countdown would detonate before then and so all delegates agreed they would contact their loved ones back home.

They now desperately needed to arrange their passages to whatever Nuclear bomb proof shelters were available.

Each delegate pleaded with their families not to mention what was happening to anyone, no matter how close they were. Survival of the fittest, echoed in their minds.

Friends, family, relatives, highly qualified engineers, scientists, doctors, pharmacists. It mattered not, for there were only so many places available in each shelter and the rations and stores were finite.

Not only that, each Zone government had already decided who would be sheltered.

Then the raw emotion of the delegates and their teams kicked in, at the real prospect of never seeing their loved ones again. Security at the summit hall was increased dramatically, and there within lay another problem. How could they possibly control several hundred security guards, who would almost certainly hear what is going on and want to leave to be with their families.

And so the chairman decided to issue a statement that with immediate effect a simulated nuclear attack scenario on Beijing would be started.

He also banned anyone other than the senior delegates from re-entering the summit hall at 4pm.

Even their entourages were to be kept in their sleeping quarters. Also a complete clamp down in and out of the summit meeting grounds was immediately started.

This was relatively easy to implement, as every Zone had practiced and practiced for the day nuclear war would break out. So they all had plans and procedures that had been perfected.

This also had to include normal daily visitors to the summit centre, plus a press and media blackout.

Within a few hours the action had been completed and the entire summit centre lay eerily silent, save the panting air conditioning units and an occasional passing by of vehicles.

Lenechka, Parveen, Monique, Dhul Fiqaar and Aaheru wandered aimlessly around the complex from room to room, to their quarters, to a restaurant, back to the summit hall. Just ambling, thinking again and again what they hade started.

And all the time living the terror that the nuclear bombs would detonate, for they had loved ones too, but they had been told not to warn or notify anyone.

In fact all up-links to the GPS system were blocked and then only re-instated for select delegates.

C'est aussi grave que les gens se

[This is as serious as it gets folks] announced Monique, but we have to see this through, though if agreed, the outcomes will be horrendous, with millions of unborns, miscarriages and population stagnation.

It would take at least five years for the world's population to reduce by 50%, and who would be able to measure and keep such a statistic. The logistics would be a nightmare.

The seemingly endless day reached 3:45pm and the delegates slowly filed back into the summit hall amidst very tight security requiring detailed checking of everyone entering.

It was 5pm before order was restored and the delegates seated. All security guards were ordered out of the hall and the soundproof double doors, locked from within.

All electricity to the hall was switched off save the domestic lighting circuits. Every delegate was asked to empty their pockets, in all clothing, and to lay any electrical device on their desks.

Nobody wanted any record of what was about to be discussed and agreed.

During the day the chairman had ordered a statistical data search of the world's population, which could only be established before the Zones were formed.

Population data records were held loosely in each Zone but quite frankly detailed and accurate records were irrelevant.

The delegates wanted commencement figures against which they could measure.

The chairman stood up, took a very deep breath and asked if he could be heard by all delegates.

When satisfied that he could be heard he signalled for a control room to activate the security scanners in the hall. These would immediately pick up on any active electrical device, even battery powered.

To the dismay and disgust of the majority of delegates several recorders were running and the offending delegates pin pointed. Summit hall senior staff went to the identified delegates desk and took their devices from them. These scanners, declared the chairman, will now remain on, as clearly not all delegates can be trusted.

To business, he continued. We are all still alive and the nuclear bombs have not detonated.

Though I understand he said apologetically, each device is still counting down, then resetting and starting another countdown sequence. It is if these devices are playing games with us. Playing cat and mouse.

Ladies and gentlemen, you have had time to reflect on what the Facilitators said this morning. It seems as if there is no alternative but to actively and deliberately introduce a formal programme of global population control by 50% at today's estimated level, which is, he said hesitantly, 9 billion souls.

He turned to the massive projector screen and signalled for a presentation to commence. Flickering lights danced around the screen as the focus went in and out, leaving a table of numerical values.

Though dating back over twenty years the tables gave clear comparisons starting with the ten most populated countries. More accurately redefined into 147 Zones.

7 most populated countries (Zones)

26.8% Nigeria.

24.7% Pakistan.

16.8% Bangladesh

16.5% India.

13.3% Indonesia.

12.25 Brazil

10.4% USA

6.9% China

2.06% Russia.

0.2% Japan

Seeing this first slide caused a premature outbreak of protestations, as the delegates felt they were being presented with 'une decison déjà fait'. No ! no ! hurriedly shouted the chairman. This is to give you as much background facts as we can, as you prepare your decision. You will be the ones to decide, not I !

The next slide bought mixes of applause and laughter and some considerable desk thumping as they reminded themselves who the host Zone was for this summit.

The 7 countries with the largest total population:

China	1,340,850,000	19.5%
India	1,190,720,000	17.3%
United States	310,793,000	4.51%
Indonesia	238,400,000	3.4%
Brazil	193,845,000	2.82%
Pakistan	171,161,000	2.49%
Bangladesh	164,425,000	2.39%
Nigeria	158,259,000	2.3%
Russia	141,927,297	2.06%
Japan	127,380,000	1.85%

Approximately 53% of the world's population live in these countries.

The chairman continued with another statistic. That of a continuing growth rate of 1.14% per year. In ten years he soberly calculated, the world would have nearly 10 billion souls to house, feed and support.

The next table gave countries ranking in the top both in terms of total population (more than 20 million people) and population density (more than 300 people per square kilometre):

Rank Country	Population	Density)
1. India	1,190,720,000	3,287,240
2. Bangladesh	157,813,124	143,998
3. Japan	127,170,110	377,873

4. Philippines	93,843,460	300,076
5. Vietnam	85,789,573	331,689
6. U.K.	62,041,708	243,610
7. South Korea	49,354,980	99,538
8. Taiwan	22,955,395	35,980
9. Sri Lanka	20,238,000	65,610
10. Netherlands	16,630,000	41,526

Initially these tables seemed pointless to most. But then the awful realisation came to them.

This was not going to be a globally equal reduction of populations, but exterminations of whole Zones. This would then be coupled with population control in the remaining Zones.

This remarkable, sickening proposition was mind blowing and equated to ethnic cleansing, the holocaust , the Ku Klux Klan and the sum total of man's inhumanity to their fellow man.

Lenechka, Parveen, Monique, Dhul Fiqaar and Aaheru squirreled away in the wings of the great hall,

listening intently. Wondering if they had been discarded having started this evil ball rolling or would they be returned to centre stage for more explanation and justification.

The next three hours continued with slide after slide of statistical data on populations. It was as if this relentless bombardment of numbers would or could justify the eventual outcome.

Destroy whole Zones and the chemical stoppage of all pregnancies that would be applied to every Zone, irrespective.

The fact that the elite in each Zone would simply avoid the national water supplies and continue having children was understood, but never mentioned. Again the sickening hypocrisy of mankind.

By 10pm all were exhausted but too tense to relax. Copious amounts of alcohol were consumed after a light supper as the delegates huddled into groups.

The chairman had made it perfectly clear that there would never be a unanimous outcome, so a majority rule would be sought and accepted. No matter how marginal that majority.

All reconvened the next day at 10am, amidst much speculation on what the outcome would be this fateful day. A day that would mark how mankind failed his own species and then took the most awful decision.

The chairman invited the Facilitators to add any comment they thought appropriate.

Parveen was tempted, for she was riddled with guilt and confusion. But it would only be repetition and these delegates clearly have enough on their minds. So the Facilitators remained silent.

The chairman called for inputs from the delegates floor but surprisingly few had any comment to make, seeking mainly to confirm their options.

However many did ask for the proposals to be formally defined and documented. And so it was agreed this fateful day, two options with no variants would be tabled and submitted.

A)   The total elimination of selected Zones with the elite from those Zones being granted free and unrestricted passage to any Zone they chose. The balance of the population containment programme would be chemical cessation of all pregnancies.

B) All Zones would be subject to the population containment programme, for the masses, through the pharmaceutical abortifacients programme.

A) or B). No variant or compromise allowed and definitely no abstaining. To help ensure this happens every delegate would be asked to walk to a counting table located in the hall, to take a simply plain slip and to write on it A or B., their name and Zone.

The count would only start when every delegate had voted. No delegate would be allowed to leave the great hall until a final vote was announced by the chairman.

The next two hours were timeless and endless. Their votes cast, each had now to consider the two outcomes and then whichever one prevailed.

The world would reach the 50% population target much quicker if the elimination route were taken. But the awful, terrifying prospect of millions of corpses needing to be gathered up and placed in mass graves. And for those who somehow evaded or escaped the death sentence, how would these be treated. Rounded up by death squads and executed jeered several delegates.

Good grief this nightmare was actually playing out. The votes were being counted. How could this have gone so far. Pinch me for this has to be a bloody dream. Written, directed, produced and played out by the Devil.

If this goes through we have all descended into hell. If only there was a God to whom we could turn. But any form of a God is a redundant concept, inconsequential and impotent. That had been proved, time and again.

Inspired by the book "Inferno", the first book of Dante Aligheri's epic poem " The Divine Comedy" This takes you on nightmarish journey into the nine circles of hell to save the soul of his beloved Beatrice from Lucifer, who needs to marry a heaven-bound soul to be able to break free from his prison and make another attempt to overthrow God.

Dante's quest takes you through many monstrous & demonic enemies within the nine circles of Hell to save Beatrice, along the way, Dante must face his own sins, His family's past, and his war crimes.

This classical teaching runs through the turmoil led consciences of so many of the delegates.

At 11pm the chairman calls everyone to order. A result has been reached. The atmosphere was electric as high emotion permeated the static air.

To everyone's amazement delegates were holding hands. Some with head in their hands. Others unable to sit still. Goodness could this be that these soulless policy makers were human after all.

Like a high court judge about to pass the death sentence on some pathetic prisoner, the chairman's grieved countenance gave a hesitant A) yes, that's right option A) it was to be.

A)   The total elimination of selected Zones with the elite from those Zones being granted free and unrestricted passage to any Zone they chose. The balance of the population containment programme would be chemical cessation of all pregnancies, for the masses only, not the elite.

Chapter 11.
The Consequences

The total elimination of selected Zones with the elite from those Zones being granted free and unrestricted passage to any Zone they chose. The balance of the population containment programme across the remaining Zones, would be chemical cessation of all pregnancies, of the masses only, through public water.

This death sentence would haunt the delegates for the rest of their lives. For any act of such magnitude in the elimination of millions of people cannot rest easy on any conscience. No matter what justification is attached to the decision.

Every delegate had been asked to identify eight Zones whose total populations would be eliminated.

Only two voting delegates allowed for each Zone, giving two hundred and ninety four votes.

The chairman ordered three re-counts, each time with different referees. The whole process took a day and once again the delegates shuffled back into the summit hall, to hear the fateful outcome.

The chairman confirmed the remit for all delegates. He explained precisely how the count had been formalised and repeated. He was pre-empting, as far as possible, the inevitable outcry and backlash.

With a hesitant, shaking voice he announced the condemned Zones. There were cries of disbelief as Zone after Zone was announced. Those are,

Country name Zone.		**Designated Zones**
India	093	
Bangladesh	076	
Philippines	059	
Vietnam	128	
Sri Lanka	111	
Nigeria.	067	
Pakistan.	132	
Indonesia.	099	

The chairman had also asked the delegates for a list of supervising Zones who will ensure the mass extermination is completed in every respect.

This would involve military intervention if any of the condemned Zones did not carry through.

		Supervising Zones.
USA.	001	
France	047	
Germany.	131	
China	008	
UK,	004	
Russia	005	
Egypt	108	
Canada.	009	
Brazil	012	
Australia	057	
South Africa.	022	

As the awful facts were considered by the delegates then those from the condemned Zones started questioning the whole process of selection and sentencing.

But the more they protested the firmer the chairman became. The results are irreversible.

Understandably the delegates were totally pre-occupied with the sentenced Zones, no thought being given to the chemical intervention that would follow the mass extermination, to drastically curtail the size of the future human race.

The nuclear bombs, the chairman was constantly advised, continued the infuriating countdown, resetting and starting again. A cyclic death threat, that no one dare challenge.

The five Facilitators, Aaheru, Lenechka, Parveen, Monique and Dhul Fiqaar, sought solace and comfort from their raging consciences, defaulting to each other's strained company.

But there was nothing to say. No appropriate or relevant reason for exoneration, but did they deserve this anguish. Yes, no. oh! Christ I don't know. Minds in a tail-spin. Out of control.

They sat as a pitiful group of exhausted people, trying to drown their sorrows with the finest cognac in the summit centre. Kept on drinking until they all felt ill. Still no respite.

They left the drinks bar around midnight and staggered to their sleeping quarters, under the watchful eye of their bodyguards, who by now fully understood what had been decided.

Four of the ten bodyguards nervously asked the Facilitators if they could be allowed to return home for they came from, or had loved ones in, the sentenced Zones and wanted to protect them.

This was a real dilemma for if they returned home and the word got out regarding the impending mass extermination, then absolute chaos would follow, in those Zones.

These bodyguards had literally risked their lives to protect the Facilitators without ever asking for anything. And now at this critical time, they ask for what is a perfectly reasonable request.

In fact all the bodyguards had become restless and Aaheru, Lenechka, Parveen, Monique and Dhul Fiqaar knew the world was soon to be turned on its head, with unimaginable consequences.

The Facilitators called a meeting with the bodyguards to fully discuss the situational options.

All fifteen sat down, for the first time as equals. It seemed strange and yet perfectly correct for the protected and the protectors to be together in this way, at this time.

The exchanges not surprisingly were emotional and tense. If the Facilitators refused to allow their bodyguards to go home, would the bodyguards then not simply revolt and leave anyway.

The terrible truth, known only to Facilitators, is that any bodyguard can be instantly killed, for during training they had, unknowingly been injected with a death capsule.

The reason. Quite simple. If ever a bodyguard turned on a Facilitator the Facilitator could activate the death capsule through their communicator handset. Paralysis and death would follow in seconds.

A precaution that had never been needed for the reputation of Facilitators and their bodyguards was renown the world over as indestructible and never open to question.

The early establishment of the Facilitators and their bodyguards had caused considerable grief and death, as extremists in many Zones tried to buck the system. Within two years and several totally uncompromising events, the world got the message. The Facilitators were to be obeyed, or else.

And now Aaheru, Lenechka, Parveen, Monique and Dhul Fiqaar sat there with these guys and had to make a decision like this. To hell with it, fuck it !!. Can any of you bodyguards stay with us, and for those who can, we promise you that as soon as we can leave, you will leave with us.

The outcome. Five bodyguards were willing to stay with them but did seek re-assurance that they would in fact leave with the Facilitators. This resulted in a direct hand shake with each of them.

The departing five gave so untypical embraces to each other. These men normally would barely smile and absolutely not show any emotion. Here they were, in embrace, close to tears. An incredibly rare sight.

Aaheru, Lenechka, Parveen, Monique and Dhul Fiqaar returned to the summit hall to catch up with the latest developments.

As soon as they entered the great hall they could taste the atmosphere, it was so palpable. Women were crying, men shouting or just sat in numbed disbelieve, heads in hands, at what was being not only discussed but being arranged for execution.

The wanton annihilation of over two billion people, such a thought was explosive.

Even trying to think of it a Zone at a time, they kept visualising mountains of rotting corpses.

Men, women and children. It really was too much for many and the hall soon emptied, leaving behind only those incapable of feelings. The hard nosed, lifeless bastard pragmatists.

The chairman called an end to this the most terrible day, the world had ever known. Commentary on what happened that evening and night does not bear consideration. As each delegate went through their own hell. The next day the chairman wanted firm decisions on the methods to be employed in the mass elimination.

Once the killing started it had to be maintained at an alarming rate. For as soon as people realised what was happening there would be purgatory.

Poison the water supplies, followed by pharmaceutical abortifacients which will be happening to those surviving this nightmare, the second part of this horror. Too slow and unpredictable, many delegates argued.

Sarcastic cries of "what the hell do you suggest, firing squads" ?

Emotions were running very high which even resulted in violence between several opposing delegates who felt they were loosing their minds.

What about those nomadic people and those living in the countryside feeding off the lands and drinking from mountain streams. Then those living on remote islands, those living at sea, those travellers exploring their own Zones. So many combinations of problems.

The more they talked, the nearer they came to only one terrible truth. They had to bomb the Zones with tactical nuclear and chemical weapons. Multiple weapons deployment all with minutes. Saturation attack on all eight Zones, all on the same day.

This would require a combination of short to medium range missiles and bomber aircraft.

There will even be a call for helicopters for mountain ranges and inaccessible places.

The attack aircraft had to come from the supervising Zones which would mean killing other military personnel. For there was absolutely no way the military of the condemned Zones would kill their own people. More likely they would use their weapons of war against other Zones, in defence or retaliation.

It also has to be remembered that many of the condemned Zones had highly sophisticated nuclear weapons that could cause incredible devastation.

The planning for this elimination had to be so very precisely managed and it was agreed this would fall to the military in Beijing.

The incredible control and management shown by the chairman contributed greatly to this decision.

Reports had been received that the 'Press' and other media outlets had infiltrated the summit and had attempted to relay this news back to their Zones.

Their communications had been tracked and intercepted or jammed and the offending individuals taken away for interrogation and incarceration. For certain they would not be seen or heard of again.

Aaheru, Lenechka, Parveen, Monique and Dhul Fiqaar had agreed with their respective Zone leaders and attending delegates that they would leave Beijing within 48 hours. They had their own plans and arrangements to make. They could not engage in the debate about how the elimination would actually work. That was for the professional war merchants and their henchmen.

Heavily encrypted instructions had already started back to the Ministries of the supervising Zones.

Despite the terrible things to follow, there seemed a strange tranquillity as they met for the evening meal, still keeping to themselves, declining invitations from the delegates.

Small talk, some reminiscing, day dreaming, cracking jokes, it all came out as they dined.

Will pack our bags tomorrow they thought, and then home. Christ it can't come soon enough and yet, the awful torment about the Presence and the eight thermal nuclear bombs still on cyclic priming.

Parveen and Monique still harboured a very strong desire for one last attempt at contacting the Presence. They knew better than to share that with Aaheru, Lenechka, and Dhul Fiqaar least they be ridiculed or actively dissuaded.

So they agreed to meet some three hundred metres behind their sleeping quarters that very evening after the meal. "Coming for a drink", invited the male facilitators "giving it a miss", the girls replied.

It was just before midnight when two heavily coated Facilitators met, full with nervous apprehension.

They paced up and down not knowing what the hell they should say or do, thinking bizarrely that the Presence would just appear and make a meaningful communication. How bloody naïve they thought but neither would comment.

An hour passed and they were extremely cold, when it happened. That eerie feeling, frightening but not in a way that they feared for their safety. A look of realisation passed between them, as they reached out for each other. They could most definitely sense the Presence. It was with them, close by, it had to be. Still they could see or hear nothing. But they knew, they had made contact even though superficial.

Now, can they communicate, speech or telepathy.

They looked absolutely pathetic standing there arm in arm exhaling steamy breath into the night air.

Try as they might there was no way they were going to be able to communicate with the Presence.

Two hours had passed since they arrived and absolutely nothing to show for their ambition and efforts.

They looked at each, shrugged and walked, still arm in arm, back to their sleeping quarters. Comments from the bodyguards and fellow Facilitators, fell on deaf ears.

They were disillusioned and dejected for they knew the opportunities for contacting this evasive Presence were passing quickly.

Soon they would be homeward bound and the terrors of the elimination of the eight Zones would commence.

Both girls lay weary and unsettled heads on their pillows, and tried too hard to go to sleep.

Classic quandary. Need sleep, want sleep, but the mind keeps going over and over, refusing to let go.

As evasive as sleep felt, they eventually drifted off and entered that wonderful world of dream state.

Where reality acquiesces to the idiosyncrasies of the wild and unaccountable imagination.

Just one more of these, thought Monique, as she stepped carefully into the shower. She was starting to long for her loveless, but familiar apartment.

The drapes and Monet pictures now held a fascination, never forthcoming when they are daily acquaintances. Overly familiar to the point of contempt and indifference, but once taken, how the yearning returns.

You know what, we are so bloody fickle and wearisome she thought, but as she redressed mankind in her summary condemnation, her mind took another path.

Were these random thoughts or a structured, carefully conceived and executed implantation.

Whatever the cause, the fact was screaming at her.

The eight thermal nuclear bombs were all located and had been from the beginning in the eight condemned Zones, now sentenced to elimination.

The possibility of a complete coincidence, to absurd to contemplate. Fuck ! this was always meant to be.

We are playing out some sick joke masterminded by someone or something. Too profound to contemplate.

Monique hurried the other four Facilitators and their bodyguards into an annex, to ensure total privacy.

She explained what was by now obvious to them, with the siting of the bombs and the activities that led up to today. From the vagaries of the uranium that became ^{235}U and eventually bombs.

Yes 'and by the way the eight nuclear bombs had de-activated and stopped'

Has this always been the master plan, with us being fed in like mindless pawns. Wide, empty eyes, gave their reply, absolutely speechless.

Never had any of them felt so blessed useless, a big come down from their usual demigod status.

After all they had gone through before and during this event and to end up with such a devastating prognosis for mankind, was heartbreaking.

That terrible moment, when you do the deed, like Paul Tibbetts, the B-29 bomber pilot who dropped the atomic bomb on Hiroshima killing eighty thousand people instantly and by 1945, a total of one hundred and forty thousand people, through radiation poisoning.

After the mission Mr. Tibbetts said: "If Dante had been with us on the plane, he would have been terrified. The city we had seen so clearly in the sunlight a few minutes before was now an ugly smudge. It had completely disappeared under this awful blanket of smoke and fire."

All eight thermal nuclear bombs had been under constant guard and scrutiny. All eight had functioned in exactly the say way, at the same time and now all eight were in standby mode.

Airports in and around Beijing were busily arranging for the many delegates and their entourages to go home.

The mass exodus was quite remarkable when you consider, what was to now happen.

Within weeks word was received that the elimination of the eight Zones would commence in 48 hours.

There had been frantic activity as the elite from the condemned Zones made good their escape, to what was now friendly Zones. Already change was underway, people were talking, sharing concerns, offering help, embracing life.

The logistical nightmare of how to carry out the death sentence in the eight condemned Zones was reckless but had to be managed because of radioactive fallout and contamination from toxins.

The decision had been made for enforced, global, population reduction. The next consideration was the terrible dilemma of how and when. The sentenced Zones having already been decided, though supposedly, only their Zone leaders knew. But for how long ?

What will be the weapons and the delivery systems, for the mass destruction.

The difficulties associated with tactile nuclear weapons were manifest and very difficult for any measure of certain control. Poisoned water supplies could take weeks maybe months to eliminate complete populations. There would be stragglers and opportunistic survivors, who could create revengeful havoc.

Chemical warfare equally had a high random factor because of the constantly changing and totally unpredictable weather patterns, unless ground zero detonations could be achieved. But then which chemicals and how would the terrain be effected, in terms of future cultivation and habitation.

In desperation the Zone leaders once again turned to the annuals of history to identify what man made atrocities and natural disasters had the maximum impact through loss of life. The final solution had to be able to eliminate tens of millions of people in a very short period of time, and before hostile retaliation could start.

The solution came from the Minister of the Environment from Zone 142. Korea.

He reasoned that such a deliberate atrocity had to appear as if absolutely not man made, or influenced, in order to succeed. For hundreds of years, well before Zonalisation, natural disasters around the globe had been accepted as inevitable. A 'man versus nature' endless battle, with nature, always winning.

What catastrophic phenomenon, even though man made, could be made to look as if it was a natural occurrence, and it had to occur in a total of eight Zones. The Environmental Minister's name was Dae-Hyun, a name that would stay in history until the end of time.

His idea: to create Firestorms whilst poisoning.

He explained to his anxious and bemused colleagues that Firestorms are conflagrations which attain such intensity that they create and sustain their own wind systems. Though most commonly a natural phenomenon, created during some of the largest bushfires, forest fires, and wildfires. Sometimes the conflagration produces a firestorm, in which the central column of rising heated air induces strong inward winds, which supply oxygen to the fire. His plan was to create firestorms, as the deliberate effects of targeted explosives. Historically the devastating effect of created firestorms were evidenced following aerial bombings of Dresden and Tokyo, during World War II. (1939 – 1945). His plan made those atrocities look insignificant.

Nuclear detonations invariably generate firestorms of far greater devastation and though radioactive fallout is unavoidable, these devices now had to be considered.

Smoke from forest fires contain tiny particles (aerosols) produced when a fire incompletely burns through trees and other carbon-based fuel. These aerosols usually linger in the lower part of the atmosphere before falling out but can be lifted to great altitudes. If sufficiently high air temperatures can be generated then these particles should re-ignite and compound the firestorm effect.

Another major factor must be to ensure that only populated areas are subject to the firestorms. It would be absolutely pointless to create and direct firestorms over mountain ranges, open countryside, rivers, estuaries, sparsely populated regions. And yet the firestorm fuel found in forests and jungles are essential components.

The physicists required to calculate the weapons and delivery systems, the distribution patterns, the amount of natural firestorm fuel already existing, the additional fuels required to be delivered, the prevailing and changing wind patterns, ground and air temperatures on the days of detonation, ground condition for moisture contents particularly if there has been a drought, or recent flooding.

The use of limited tactical nuclear devices must have totally controlled impact and fallout for heat wave, blinding light, push-pull air pressure waves and radioactive fallout. Intensity depends of weapon grade, size, ground or air detonation.

The extreme difficulties associated with the disposal of so many corpses was a major concern. The only possible solution was to create disasters' in each Zone in such a fashion that actually encouraged the remaining population to make the arrangements for mass burials.

Then as the disasters continued, the diminishing population would assume the task of corpse disposal, aided by other so-called friendly Zones. Except the friendly Zones would never commit their own people into the killing Zones.

The irony was unthinkable as the rapidly diminishing population in each targeted Zone was seemingly aided, unbeknown, by their own executers. The supervising Zones under the control of the Beijing Government, progressively and systematically reducing the world's population by fifty percent.

All the time retaining the fertility of the land and water systems, for continuing occupation by humans and animals. Many Zone leaders would not, could not comprehend what had been agreed and sanctioned. These were the weakest links.

Many suicides followed. Some self evident, others highly suspicious, as certain Ministers, riddled with a conscience, tried to tell the world what had been agreed. But as soon as any 'notoriety', as they were called, was outspoken, they would soon disappear and their claims publicly ridiculed.

Despite the immense, intense preparatory efforts, all those directly involved knew it would hinge on the first wave of attacks and the reactions that follow.

It had been decided that the weapons to be used would be a combination of Tactical Nuclear, Biological and Chemical, without defoliants.

Short term or immediate impact would come from tactile nuclear weapons.

Mid term fatalities from Biological weaponry through the use of biological agents such as protozoa, fungi, bacteria, protists, or viruses, all are living organisms or replicating entities that reproduce within their host victims. The effects would be devastating.

Longer term fatalities came from the side effects of all three destructive systems.

The precise combinations would be decided on a Zone by Zone basis but to hold onto any precarious credibility, firestorms would remain the central component.

Notification of the impending firestorm potential would be given as metrological warnings issued to the world as a precursor to the deliberate commencement of the firestorms.

It would be vital that most of the world became convinced that nature was the only reason for the firestorms that would lead to such unprecedented catastrophe.

The propaganda Ministries of many of the supervising Zones were working closely on this massive misinformation programme.

Since the formation of the Zones, information sharing had stopped, however it would be argued that for humanitarian reasons these impending weather patterns would be globally publicised. The announcements would be given with dire warnings.

A Red Flag Warning forecast system had been established by the United States National Weather Service, to inform area firefighting and land management agencies that conditions are ideal for wildland fire ignition and propagation. After drought conditions, and when humidity is very low, and especially when high or erratic winds which may include lightning, are a factor.

The Red Flag Warning becomes a critical statement for firefighting agencies, which often alter their staffing and equipment resources dramatically to accommodate the forecast risk. To the public, a Red Flag Warning means high fire danger with increased probability of a quickly spreading vegetation fire in the area.

The criteria for fire weather watches and red flag warnings varies with each Weather Service Office's warning area, based on the local vegetation type, topography, and distance from major water sources. This usually includes the daily vegetation moisture content calculations, expected afternoon high temperature, afternoon minimum relative humidity and daytime wind speed.

Outdoor burning bans may also be proclaimed by local law and fire agencies based on Red Flag Warnings.

This Red Flag warning would be coupled with identical warnings from The Australian Governments Bureau of Meteorology for wind, temperature, humidity and rainfall all combine to affect the behaviour of bushfires.

In Australia there is a system of assessing these in conjunction with the state of the available fuels to determine a measure of "fire danger", or the difficulty of putting out any fires which may occur. The Bureau of Meteorology issues Fire Weather Warnings to alert the public when conditions are likely to be dangerous. The Bureau also includes advices when State agencies issue Fire Bans.

The joint communiqué from these two global weather authorities would be all that was needed to start the Programme of Population Reduction. (P.P.R.)

As neither Zone had been identified as a target Zone, then co-operation was a formality. Though certain conscientious objectors had to be quickly dealt with.

To convince the populations of each targeted Zone it was important to give them something to believe in, and so the Red Flag Warnings would contain graphic illustrations of what happens in firestorms.

The propaganda statement would read:-

"Large fires create their own weather, by rapidly heating the air above them.

If the superheated air rises fast and high enough, it forms a towering thundercloud, the tops of these cauliflower-shaped clouds often reach high enough into the atmosphere, that ice crystals form.

Those ice crystals electrify the cloud, creating lightning. Called pyrocumu-lonimbus clouds, that are capable of dangerous lightning, hail, and strong winds, to tornado strength.

So a pyrocumulus cloud is produced by the intense heating of the air from the surface. The intense heat induces convection which causes the air mass to rise to a point of stability, usually in the presence of moisture. Phenomena such as volcanic eruptions, forest fires, and occasionally industrial activities can induce formation of this cloud. The presence of a low level jet stream can enhance its formation.

Condensation of ambient moisture (moisture already present in the atmosphere) as well as moisture evaporated from burnt vegetation or volcanic out gassing occurs readily on particles of ash.

What would not be stated is that the detonation of tactical nuclear weapons in the atmosphere will also produce a pyrocumulus in the form of a mushroom cloud which is made by the same mechanism.

Pre-occupation with the Red Flag Warnings and the starting of the firestorms should distract ground observation teams in the targeted Zones from detecting the deployment of Biological and Chemical weapons delivery systems. Most of which would be detonated in the atmosphere, coincident with strong weather fronts.

To have a fire, two things are required, an oxidiser and fuel. There is plenty of oxidiser (Oxygen) in the atmosphere, but virtually no fuel. There's a very small amount of hydrogen, which is a fuel, but there is such a tiny amount of this & would make no difference.

It is not necessary to actually ignite the atmosphere, well not literally. What is required is a supply of fuel or materials to burn. Anything carbon based is needed, plus particulates or aerosols. The lighter the fuel the quicker it will burn out and so heavy wood lands, forests and jungles are essential.

These were very easy to identify and map and to calculate the burn cycle times, To start the firestorms was likewise simple, using incendiary bombs usually containing thermite, made from aluminium and ferric oxide. The most effective formula is 25% aluminium and 75% iron oxide. It takes very high temperatures to ignite, but when alight, it can burn through solid steel.

A variety of pyrophoric materials would also be used: Selected organo-metallic compounds, most often triethylaluminium, trimethylaluminium, and some other alkyl and aryl derivates of aluminium, magnesium, boron, zinc, sodium, and lithium.

Also thickened triethylaluminium, a napalm-like substance that ignites in contact with air, is known as thickened pyrophoric agent, or TPA.

Napalm proper though discontinued remains a consideration and the kerosene-fueled Mark 77 MOD 5 Firebomb a possibility including the use of accelerants.

A fire is a self sustaining, exothermic oxidation reaction that emits heat and light. When a fire is accelerated, it can produce more heat, consume the reactants more quickly, burn at a higher temperature, and increase the spread of the fire.

An accelerated fire is said to have a higher "heat release rate," meaning it burns more quickly.

Also to be used is Napalm B usually a mixture of the plastic polystyrene and the hydrocarbon benzene. This is used as a thickening agent to make jellied gasoline.

Napalm B has an advantage in that its ignition can be well-controlled.

Fallbrook napalm, was nevertheless the favoured choice, with a mixture of 46% of polystyrene, 33% gasoline, and 21% benzene.

This mixture though difficult to ignite can burn for up to ten minutes. Napalm 877 is formulated to burn close to a specified rate and also to adhere to surfaces.

Another deadly effect of napalm B, primarily in its use in firebombs, is that napalm "rapidly deoxygenates the available air" and it also releases large amounts of deadly carbon monoxide. For maximum impact there should always be a drought first.

Forests and heavily bush growth areas of countryside are required. Then powerful natural weather fronts with high and varying winds at least to start the firestorm.

The weather patterns, a major consideration. Streams and rivers flowing into the waterways of other Zones.

Animal migration, on land, the birds and also insects.

People not being successfully exterminated with the masses, left free to seek survival or retribution.

There is to be a combination of chemical warfare dropped by air (Chem-Trails) and introduced into the food chain and mains water supply, and bombing.

Vast amounts of these toxins and weapons had to be obtained and secretly transported and administered, without drawing any attention. No easy task.

The press and mass media in each of the condemned Zones had to be distracted. Close knit communities like the clergy, likewise kept totally in the dark.

The military would still be fully active in each of the condemned Zones, with their sophisticated defence systems. They would certainly react to the presence of the Supervising Zones aircraft and short range missiles.

Localised wars being fought were absolutely not to happen. So instructions were given to destroy military bases and all defence response capabilities, before the mass population extermination.

Back in her London apartment Monique enjoyed the trappings of being home. She had sent farewell messages to Aaheru, Lenechka, and Dhul Fiqaar, who are now life long friends. Or until Armageddon.

The extermination programme lasted for five years with sporadic fighting, and revolts and insurrections when supervising Zones refused to destroy all condemned Zones.

Civil unrest was unprecedented and many terrorist groups formed, but were quelled almost as quickly.

To this day there are survivors in the eight condemned Zones, though in such small numbers and reportedly suffering badly from radiation and chemical aftermath.

The chemical sterilisation, pharmaceutical abortifacients took even longer, estimated to be still ongoing in 2080.

The divisions in society became even more pronounced and resulted in secured community villages for the elite and sprawling housing programmes for the masses.

By 2095 it was estimated that the worlds population had reduced to 3.8 billion, a drop of nearly 6 billion from the 2060 figures. The sterilisation had been most effective.

Tens of thousands of square miles had been laid to waste not just decimated by man but equally by nature, whose oft time cruelty can put man in a good light.

With skilful engineering and genetically modified arable and livestock farming practices, the remaining lands stayed fertile. Providing more than enough to feed all of mankind, without wars, want or famine.

A measure of normality returned to a pre-2025 level. The world was seemingly rebuilding itself, as if undergoing a metamorphosis.

Nevertheless the quintessential question remained. Who or what caused this profound situation that resulted in the world's leaders taking such drastic action.

Is man so inherently flawed that he would allow ruination of the very planet that sustains him, in pursuit of greed, without ever a thought for all of mankind.

Or was there a group of people whose intellect and compassion transcended the primeval basic urges of man, to determine that most had to be saved from themselves, through controlled extermination.

Those Facilitators directly involved, their bodyguards and the Zone leaders, never spoke of the bizarre and unfathomable events that took place in 2060.

The question of extra terrestrial intervention haunted many for years, but of course, remained unanswered.

In the years that followed there were many undisclosed events that required the exclusive services of the Facilitators. Monique for one, kept a very detailed diary.

About the Author

I have always been a story teller, from my days in 20 man billets in the Royal Air Force, to bedtime stories for my children. I also write prose and dedications.

Qualifications. I believe I have the imagination, creativity and passion for story telling but as an engineer and professional manager, I maintain contact with reality.

I live in a beautiful village in Hampshire, flanked by open fields, a forest and views of the South Downs.